LUNDERSTON TALES

Lunderston Tales

Robin Jenkins

Polygon
Edinburgh

First published by
Polygon
22 George Square
Edinburgh

Copyright © Robin Jenkins 1996

Set in Galliard by Palimpsest Book Production Limited,
Polmont, Stirlingshire
Printed and bound in Great Britain by
Cromwell Press, Broughton Gifford, Melksham, Wiltshire.

A CIP record is available for this title.

ISBN 0 7486 6221 9

The Publisher acknowledges subsidy from

towards the publication of this volume.

To Brian, and Queenie
of Inverchaolin

Contents

Foreword

A scottish novelist recently complained that one of the disadvantages of belonging to his nation was that nothing ever happened in it spectacular or exciting enough to be of interest to the rest of the world. No president was assassinated, no government overthrown, no political prisoners tortured. All this is true and shows virtue or at least placidity on the part of the Scots, but one can see why a novelist would feel frustrated. A few years ago an offer, grudgingly made by the Parliament in London, of a measure of self-government, was not accepted by the Scots, on the grounds, it seemed, that it would mean their having to assume responsibility for their own destinies. The lion rampant was happier on his belly, with his paws covering his eyes.

Only on the football field nowadays do the Scots assert themselves, boasting that they are a match for any nation on earth. The belief persists, in spite of numerous defeats and few victories. In stadiums all over the world Scottish football supporters bawl their maudlin anthem *The Flower of Scotland* with the same passion with which their forebears rushed at the English at Bannockburn more than five hundred years ago. Those fanatics, however, when given the choice of staying in the pub and playing dominoes or going down the road in the rain to vote for home-rule chose the former. In brief therefore a country that, too supine to take itself seriously, does not deserve to be taken seriously by any other country. This also was what the novelist was grumbling about.

Yet, paradoxically, its individual people are as interesting as any in America or Russia. Take for example the small seaside town of Lunderston, on the Firth of Clyde. It has only nine thousand of a population. Its main industry, indeed almost its only one, is tourism, which takes the form of entertaining bus parties from the North of England. There is also an American air base not far away, which brings trade to the pubs, of which there are ten. Anyone passing through or staying overnight might remark on the scenery or the bakers' shops or the courtesy of the citizens, but they would be incredulous if they were told that in this small town, so douce and placid on the surface, with its eight churches and its pipe band recitals in front of the Burgh Hall during the season, there were to be found individuals whose lives touched upon the great issues of our times and who represented the twentieth century as much as any inhabitants of New York or Moscow. Yet it is true. With them as his material no novelist need feel parochial.

The Greengrocer and the Hero

T HE HILDERSONS CAME TO Lunderston from South
Africa; Mr and Mrs Andrew Hilderson, their daughter
Daphne aged seven, and their son Gary aged three. The
children had been born in Johannesburg and had Cockney-
sounding accents to prove it, but the parents were Scottish,
with only the faintest of outlandish twangs. So far as anyone
knew they had had no previous connection with Lunderston.
Presumably they chose it because it was a beautiful quiet little
backwater where the absence of anything sinister or violent
above or below the surface – it was just before the coming of
the Americans – must have been a great relief after the strains
of a country in which, in a manner of speaking, millions of
blacks were kept chained like dogs and one day were sure
to break loose and savage their masters. Mr Hilderson was
young to be retired from whatever his business had been
and yet he seemed to have plenty of money, for he bought
Goatfell House, one of the mansions in Ailsa Park, the very
select residential area overlooking the town. According to
their charwoman, Mrs McLean, they had it adorned with
various African objects, some of which she did not approve
of, such as wooden statues of black women whose bottoms
were much too big. What Mrs McLean also did not like was
Mrs Hilderson's habit of coming into the kitchen to have a

coffee with her. That was all right, though a bit forward of her really, but what disturbed Mrs McLean was that Mrs Hilderson kept confusing her with a servant she had had in Johannesburg called Hannah. That was all right too, except that Hannah had been coal black. Still, the wages were good, and Mr Hilderson thought nothing of running her home in his black car, a Daimler, which had all her neighbours in the council housing scheme at their windows, the first time it happened, thinking that somebody had died and this was the undertaker arriving. Lying in bed beside her husband Archie Mrs McLean once had tried to imagine Mr Hilderson thrashing a Negro with a whip. It had been so comically unlikely that she laughed aloud, to Archie's puzzlement. Mr Hilderson was one of the gentlest men she had ever met, so much so it was more of a fault than a virtue, in that he had no control over his children, especially Gary, who was allowed to do as he pleased.

It would have been an exaggeration and an injustice to call Gary Hilderson a problem child. From the age of three, when he first arrived in Lunderston, he was a 'bloody wee nuisance', to use Mrs McLean's words, echoed by many, but most people, she included, liked him none the less. It was hard to believe that any child could pay no heed to anyone's instructions or pleas, without seeming insolent, but Gary managed it with ease. As Mrs McLean told her grunting Archie, he had charm.

Refusing to be offended himself, whatever was said or done to him, Gary was readily forgiven for any offence he caused. Besides, he was a bright, happy, handsome little boy. Teachers went against their principles and made excuses for him, though one or two more percipient than the others wondered if what was wrong with him was that he did not have any instinctive notion of right and wrong. Other children accused him of stealing their pencils or comics. He would laugh and say that he had just been borrowing them.

In vain it was pointed out to him that borrowing without any intention of giving back was the same as stealing. Why should he be a thief though, when he could afford to buy all the pencils and comics he wanted? Discreetly, he was seen by a child psychologist who assured his parents and the school authorities that there was nothing to worry about. Gary had a richer and more complex personality than most children, so it was not surprising that in expressing it he should now and then indulge in unusual activities. One of those, however, caused anxiety; he hurt people, both physically and mentally, without apparently being aware of it. If it was brought to his notice that holding a magnifying glass to someone's neck on a hot day was a cruel thing to do, he would be at a loss because if it had been done to him he wouldn't have made a fuss. He would just have waited till he got a chance to do it back.

Mr Hilderson did not mix much in Lunderston society but he joined the golf club and played regularly with three members of retirement age, two ex-bankers and an ex-accountant. Lunderston was a hilly course, particularly the fourth hole. One morning while playing it he was taken ill. Brought home by his playing partners who afterwards resumed their game, for it was a fine May morning, he died three days later in bed. He was only fifty-one.

Lunderston waited to see what the stricken family would do. It was thought that they would go back to South Africa, for Mrs Hilderson was known to grumble about the expense of servants in Scotland and Daphne wasn't happy at the local Academy, where it was an embarrassment to her to find in her classes, sitting side by side with her, black boys and girls, sons and daughters of American service-men from the base. Moreover she found the air of Lunderston, which the natives called bracing, cold and debilitating. As for Gary, he was enjoying himself at school, though hardly excelling as a scholar. It didn't matter to him whether they went or stayed.

They stayed, or rather Mrs Hilderson and Gary did. Daphne finished her education at Glasgow University and then departed. That she should be willing to leave her mother, and that her mother was prepared to let her go alone, were matters discussed in tea-rooms and at bridge parties, but not too earnestly, for after all the Hildersons were incomers, for whom the town was not accountable.

Gary was sixteen when his sister went away. It was supposed at first that he had refused to go with her because he did not want to leave his mother, but it soon became known that the real reason was Sadie Rankin, daughter of Councillor Rankin, one of the town's greengrocers.

Years later, when he had become famous or infamous, according to your interpretation of the events he took part in, Gary's affair with Sadie was remembered as sad and romantic, like Romeo and Juliet's, but at the time it was generally agreed to be unfortunate, not to say disgraceful.

Sadie was a few months older than Gary but not any more academically inclined, though sharp-witted. It was said in her defence that she had been led astray by the conscienceless young rogue with the yellow curls, but those who knew her well were doubtful, Sadie had always struck them as not easily persuaded to do what she didn't want to do and what wasn't to her advantage. She was ambitious too, and having seen the inside of Goatfell House probably fancied herself as its mistress one day. In any case, whatever the ins and outs of it were, she became pregnant and Gary was the father.

The scandal involved the school and the kirk, as well as the parents of the culprits, but the whole town was interested. The headmaster impetuously expelled them both, which many considered unjust, in that the crime, if it could be called a crime, had not been committed on his premises. According to Sadie's unabashed confession to her parents, fornication had taken place in Goatfell House, on top of a lion's skin,

4

in her own bedroom in her parents' bungalow, and on the bank of the Balgie Burn, near the Episcopal church. When her mother in anguish asked why no precautions had been used Sadie shrugged and shifted the gum from one side of her mouth to the other, giving the impression that she had seen no reason to try and thwart nature's purpose. The Pope would have been pleased but not her parents, though as good Presbyterians they could not say so. When they dashed in their car up the hill to Goatfell House to share their trauma with Mrs Hilderson she refused to open the door, though Jack swore he saw her keeking at them from behind a curtain. Reached by telephone, she said curtly that she had been informed (no doubt by her unscrupulous son) that their daughter was promiscuous, so why pick on Gary? When the Rankins had recovered from the shock of that insult they interrogated Sadie again, this time determined to get the truth out of her even if they had to use thumb screws. Coolly she admitted, using words that her parents had not known she knew, that while other boys might have fingered her breasts and private parts Gary was her only penetrator. When the baby was born they would see that it had his yellow hair.

Most of Lunderston believed her, not because they thought her truthful but because they knew her to be sly and resolute, as well as small, dark, passionate, ambitious, and big-breasted. Whether or not she would make a good mother she certainly had the equipment to entice young men, especially one like Gary Hilderson who didn't give a damn for consequences.

Thanks to the efforts of old Mr Henderson, minister of the church where the Rankins and Mrs Hilderson worshipped (if her rare silent appearances could be so described) a marriage was arranged, Gary having admitted that he probably was the father. Mrs Rankin was pleased, though she pretended that she had consented for the sake of the child. Her husband made no attempt to hide his jubilation. Though his politics were more idiosyncratic than doctrinaire he made such a practice of condemning Communists and Socialists that his friends affectionately called him a wee Fascist. South Africa was one of his favourite countries. Other greengrocers might sell its produce furtively, he did it proudly. He would not, he said, have imprisoned the black leader Mandela, he would have hanged him and all troublemakers like him. So he was delighted at the prospect of having a South African son-in-law, particularly one so handsome and well-to-do.

Gary himself agreed to the marriage without fuss, and wasn't a bit flustered when Sadie's parents came home one evening earlier than expected and found him and Sadie naked in bed. 'It's all right, Annie,' the councillor whispered to his wife, after the confrontation, 'They're as good as man and wife.'

Sadie demanded and was promised a big wedding in St Cuthbert's. She would be married in white, even if she was known or even seen to be pregnant. It was just old-fashioned stupid superstition that brides had to be virgins. Mr Henderson, belonging to a kirk that moved with the times, acquiesced, but many of his parishioners were outraged.

Two weeks before the wedding Gary vanished. His mother protested that she hadn't known he was going and didn't know where he had gone. The Rankins did not believe her, though she was telling the truth. Then four days after his disappearance she had a telephone call from South Africa. It was Gary asking for money. He said he was too young to get married. He wanted to see the world and have adventures. If she saw Sadie would she convey his apologies?

She did not see Sadie, she took care not to, but she spoke to her and to her parents on the telephone. She was sorry about the child, she said, and offered to contribute towards its keep; but the marriage would have been a disaster, they all ought

6

to be glad that it hadn't taken place, even if the cancellation had come rather late.

The Rankins were not glad. Mrs Rankin had to go to the doctor for pills to stop her palpitations; she was afraid she was going to have a heart attack. Sadie at first was quiet and pale; then one evening while her parents were trying to console her she let out a prolonged scream, like a pig being slaughtered. She said nothing, just went on screaming, with her hands contorted into claws. Whose face, wondered her father, was she minded to scart? Gary's? But he was thousands of miles away. God's? He was even further. Mine, for singing his praises? Her mother's, for giving her birth? Poor Sadie during those weeks after being jilted often muttered that she wished she had never been born. They knew that, being young, she would get over it, but they had the sense not to tell her so; better let her find it out for herself.

The councillor's disappointment was as grievous as his daughter's. His hero had behaved worse than a Communist. Gary had let down not only Sadie and Sadie's family but the whole of Western civilisation. If they had known about it in the Kremlin they would have laughed. Recklessly, before witnesses, he vowed that if young Hilderson was ever to set foot in Lunderston again he, Jack Rankin, as God was his witness, would give him the thrashing he deserved. Those who heard about the threat smiled, for Jack though game was only five feet four inches in height and weighed no more than a sackful of lettuce, whereas Hilderson at sixteen was six feet and twelve stones.

The baby was safely born, a yellow-haired, blue-eyed boy, the image of his father. He was christened John after his grandfather, but Sadie insisted that one of his names be Gary, for she still hoped that Hilderson would come back one day and marry her. Mrs Hilderson did not want to see her grandson but her offer to contribute towards his keep was this time scornfully accepted. It meant that wee John was the best-dressed baby in town and was wheeled about in the most sumptuous pram. Sadie proved a devoted and conscientious mother. She did not, as her parents had feared, blame the child for its father's betrayal of her. When wee John was five and she had at last given up hope of ever seeing his father again she married Rab Fairlie, whose family had been farmers in the district for generations. He was considered a good catch, since he was heir to five hundred fertile acres. Having led many a cow to the bull he had a relaxed attitude towards paternity and found no difficulty in accepting the little bastard as his own, and even less in providing him with a half-sister, and then, with all possible speed, with two more half-sisters and a half-brother.

In her big house Mrs Hilderson became a recluse. It was noticed by the postman that she received letters now and then from far-off parts of the world, judging from the stamps. It was assumed that these were from Gary, but where he was or what he was doing Lunderston did not know and did not really care, until one day more than ten years after his jilting of Sadie Rankin, now Sadie Fairlie.

The Melanesia affair had been in the newspapers and every night on television before Lunderston realised that it was personally involved. Sensational events in distant places were seldom the occasion for debate or discussion in the town. Lunderstonians preferred to talk about people and matters nearer to home, such as the deaths of acquaintances or increases in the rates. This was not to say that they took no intelligent interest in the world-shaking happenings reported in big black headlines. They read about them, they watched them on television, and gave them two or three minutes' silent cogitation, but they never felt compelled to rush out into the street and argue about them with passers-by. They had not come up the Clyde on bicycles. They knew that next week there would be another world-shaking happening somewhere else, and the week after that still another. Therefore they took them cannily. This particular one was the attempt by a band of mercenaries to kill the President and topple the Marxist government of a small island in the Indian Ocean.

They had flown in a chartered plane from South Africa. That country was denying any responsibility but nobody was believing it. They had come armed with automatic rifles and grenades. Exiles from the island, political enemies of the present government, had financed the venture and had promised large rewards if it succeeded; £100,000 per man was quoted. Unfortunately for the adventurers the information given to them beforehand turned out to be false. They had been assured that as soon as they appeared the people would rise up in rebellion against their oppressors, who had had the arrogance not only to promise to take from the rich and give to the poor but also had carried it out. The poor, it was thought, recognising the immorality of that redistribution, would be eager to get rid of the Communistic clique who had perpetrated it. The poor, however, being not well educated, for the previous government had been content to keep them illiterate, had not understood that the reforms which they thought were improving their lives were really destroying the economy of the island. Therefore, instead of welcoming the would-be liberators, they furiously attacked them. So did the tiny army. There was a battle at the airport. The invaders were besieged in the control tower. After three days they surrendered, having learned that there was no death penalty on the island, this having been abolished by the tyrants. It was admitted, in very small print, by most British newspapers, that the Marxists themselves had not seized power but had been democratically voted into it. The so-called liberators therefore were actually terrorists. Nevertheless to anyone reading between the lines, and Lunderstonians were as good at that as anyone, it was clear that the only fault found with them by the governments of South Africa, the United States, and Great Britain was that they had ineptly failed.

Eventually the names and photographs of the mercenaries were published. One was Gary Hilderson, of South Africa the media said, but Lunderston knew better. Gary had no mother in that country, and no son either.

Jack Rankin was briskly weighing out three pounds of Kerr's Pinks for old Mrs Brotherow when she broke the news to him, in her gruff voice that was heard all over the shop. 'I see there's a picture of a freen' of yours in this morning's paper, Jack.'

'D'you tell me?' said Jack, laughing. 'What paper's that then?'

'The *Herald*, but I expect it's in them a'. Would you like to see it?' She pulled out the *Glasgow Herald* from her shopping bag and finding the right page showed it to him, so that it was with his hands full of Kerr's Pinks that Jack looked and saw, smiling at him with well-remembered impudence, the father of his favourite grandson.

'He's one of them that tried to tak ower from the Communists on that island,' said Mrs Brotherow, 'and made a mess of it. I'll have twa pounds of Brussel sprouts as well. It says they'll get ten years in jile.'

White as a cauliflower, Jack said nothing. Just a few days ago, at a meeting of the Business Club, he had let it be known that he was in sympathy with the heroic liberators and very much hoped they succeeded. Now that enthusiasm had had a bucketful of cold disillusionment poured over it.

For the rest of the morning his heart wasn't in the selling of potatoes and sprouts. He had to go into the back shop and, amidst the smell of over-ripe pears, take a couple of paracetamol tablets, to calm the nerves in his stomach. His mind was spinning like a peerie.

When he went home at lunch-time his wife Annie met him at the door with their own copy of the *Herald*. 'Have you seen this?'

'Aye.'

'Who showed it to you?'

'Mrs Brotherow.'

'She would. Well, as you can see he's still laughing at us.'

'God knows when that was taken.'

'I'll tell you this, Jack Rankin, if they lib him like Rab does his male lambs I'll be mair than pleased.'

Rab did it with his teeth. Maybe the blacks on the island would use a knife. But it wasn't likely. They weren't as savage as all that.

Reading what it said under the photographs Jack learned that South Africa had suggested that the adventurers be sent back there to be tried. Well, South African jails being what they were there was a good chance that Hilderson would be forced to jump out of an eighth-storey window, on to solid concrete below. But did that apply only to blacks? Jack's mind was still spinning.

'And you were singing their praises,' jeered Annie, as they ate their lunch. 'Heroes of our age, you called them.'

'How was I to know he was one of them?'

'I'm worried about Sadie. He's still the one she fancies, you know.'

'You're wrong, Annie. She's got over him long ago. It's wee John we should worried about. Somebody's bound to tell him that that grinning eedjit's his real faither.'

'You can see the likeness.'

They would all see it.

'Do you think he'll get paid that £100,000?'

'They didn't succeed, did they?'

11

'But they tried, they did their best. Two of them were killed. Pity he wasn't one of them. If he does get the money wee John should get a share.'

'Wouldn't that be acknowledging that Hilderson's got rights over the boy?'

'He's got nae rights but he's got responsibility. What use will the money be to him in jail?'

'He'll not be in jail long. In South Africa they'll not be classed as criminals. They'll get sentenced to five years maybe, to kid the rest of the world. They'll be set free in six months or less. That's how it'll be done, Annie.'

She was used to Jack's telling her how it was done, as if he was Prime Minister and not a small-town greengrocer.

'If he *was* your son-in-law, Jack, you'd be proud of him, wouldn't you? Him killing Communists.'

'I expect I would. That's the only way to get rid of Reds.'

'They weren't got rid of. And an innocent woman was killed.'

'That was just propaganda.'

'It showed her body on television. It said she had six weans.'

'It didn't show who killed her, did it?'

'They were the ones started it.'

'In war accidents happen.'

'It wasn't war. They were being paid for it. It was just a job for them, like selling fruit is for you.'

He sighed. Annie would never understand. 'Are you going to phone Sadie?'

'You know she doesn't see the paper till late at night, after a' her work's done.'

It was too much for her, her work. Moreover she was pregnant again. Rab, he reflected bitterly, could do with libbing himself.

'She should have told the boy long ago that Rab isn't his
real father.'

Other children had told him. He had come home weeping.
Sadie had had to reassure him with lies.

'Well, she'll have to tell him now, after a' this publicity.
What about that crazy woman in Goatfell House? She'll no'
ken about this. They say she gets no newspaper and hasn't a
television.'

'To hell with her. It's our Sadie who concerns me. I'm
wondering how she'll take it.'

Later that night Sadie arrived at their house with an
expression on her face that they were all too familiar with.
From the age of three she had often looked fiercely revengeful
like this. They assumed that it was Hilderson who had
provoked her this time, but they were wrong, it was they
themselves, her loving and caring parents. Before they could
offer her a cup of tea she began a screaming tirade. At first
they thought it was Hilderson she was blaming for ruining
her life, and though she was exaggerating they were ready
to sympathise with her. Then it dawned on them that they
were the ones being accused. If it hadn't been for them, she
yelled, she would have married Gary and would have had a
wonderful exciting life with him in South Africa and other
sunny places instead of being buried alive in a wet hole of a
farm with a man that thought he was a bull.

If she had shed tears they would have known that it was her
emotions speaking, but she remained dry-eyed, and they saw
to their horror that she meant it, every single bitter word: it
must have been pent up in her for the past ten years.

'For God's sake, Sadie, think of your weans,' said her
mother, pouring petrol on to the flames.

Trust Annie to say the wrong thing, thought Jack, but what
was the right thing?

At last Sadie grew quieter but not any more reasonable.

She would go to Gary, she said. Mrs Hilderson would give her the money. She would visit him in prison. She would take photographs of wee John and show them to him. She would tell him that she would wait for him to come out of prison, even if it took ten more years.

You're forgetting the wean in your wame, thought her father, but he did not say it and hoped that Annie wouldn't say it either.

But Annie did, tartly. She had decided it was time to answer back. 'They don't let women as far gone as you are, Sadie, on to planes. And I'd be obliged if you'd be more fair to your faither and me. The marriage was all arranged, in case you don't remember. We arranged it, your faither and me, though we baith thought you were too young. It wasn't us that ran away, it wasn't us that left you in the lurch. We've a' had our disappointments. There was a boy in Greenock once – but I won't go into that. His father was a foreman in Scott Lithgow's.'

And there was a girl in Lochgilphead with red hair, thought Jack.

'Life's like that, Sadie,' said her mother. 'We want to gang doon one road, it sends us doon anither. It happens to us a'. Rab's no' a bad husband, though no' as bright as we would like. His coos having calves every year and his sheep lambs seems to have given him the idea that his wife should have weans just as often, but you could hae put a stop to that if you'd kept on the pill.'

For God's sake, woman, hold your tongue, prayed Jack. Luckily Sadie wasn't listening to her mother. But then who ever listened to anybody?

A few minutes later Sadie left. Her last words were quiet enough but they terrified her parents. 'I think I'll go up and see Mrs Hilderson.'

She slammed the door behind her.

'Do you think she will?' asked Annie.

'God knows.'

'That's no answer, Jack. He knows all right but He never says. I asked *you*. Will she go and see Mrs Hilderson?'

'How do I know? All right, I don't think she will. She went once before, didn't she, and was left standing on the doorstep.'

'This time they've got something to talk about.'

They didn't find out until years later whether or not Sadie went that night and talked to Mrs Hilderson.

The one good thing that came out of the crisis was that wee John learned at last who his real father was. He wasn't a bit shattered. On the contrary, he was thrilled. He liked his stepfather and indeed wanted to be a farmer like him when he grew up, but it was a lot more exciting having a father who was like a hero in a film. It was no good other boys jeering that the adventure had failed. A failed adventurer with grenades in his pocket and an automatic rifle over his shoulder was far more interesting as a father than any successful plumber or joiner. When he was older, wee John told them, he was going to call himself by his true name, John Hilderson. He too would go to dangerous places and kill Communists.

Jack Rankin proved to be right in thinking that Hilderson and his confederates would not be kept in prison long. After six months they were all let out. There were pictures of them on television celebrating with champagne. Asked if they were planning any similar missions some of them replied that wherever there was an atheistic Communist dictatorship that was a place they would like to go to bring freedom to the people. Hilderson, however, laughed and said, 'Why not, if the money's good?' He was seen and heard saying it in dozens of countries, including the United States. As a result an anti-Communist organisation there invited him to

15

do a lecture tour. There would be a lot of money in it for him, and since he was young, handsome, white, and brave he would be idolised in and out of bed by rich women. It was, a cynical journalist wrote, an enviable assignment, a fitting reward for a hero of the West. In the Scottish press it was reported with pride that on his way to America he intended to visit his mother, who lived in the small seaside town of Lunderston. It said nothing about his visiting his son, because as yet only in Lunderston was it known that he had one.

Lunderston debated as to how he should be greeted. Some said with public plaudits, one or two with rotten eggs, but the majority came to the opinion that no particular notice should be taken of him, let him enjoy his visit to his mother in peace and then depart. After all it wasn't as if he'd been born in the town, and it ought not to be forgotten that he had treated Councillor Jack Rankin's daughter despicably. At a meeting of the District Council one of its crassest members proposed that there should be a civic reception for 'a man who, whatever his faults, had struck a blow on behalf of democracy and freedom.' He looked to Councillor Rankin for his seconder and was amazed to be given a scowl quite Stalinish in its malevolence. Being from another town he had no interest in what went on in Lunderston and did not know that Councillor Rankin's grandson was also Hilderson's son. The proposal was not seconded. As someone pointed out, since the council had had to close public lavatories as an economy measure, it ought not to squander money on entertaining a man who, according to reports in the newspapers, would have at least half a million dollars showered on him in America.

Jack and Annie Rankin hoped that Hilderson would arrive in the town unannounced, spend a day or two with his mother, and then leave discreetly; but no, there he was, one evening, on Scottish television, being interviewed after the Scottish news, a programme that most of Lunderston watched. The interviewer, a young woman with a gaudy blouse and purple mouth, was evidently charmed by the tall, fair-haired, bronzed adventurer in the tan suit. The questions she put to him were innocuous, except for one, and this he answered with a humility that not everyone thought genuine, such as Mrs Rankin, who cried 'The hypocrite!' 'Did he not regret that an innocent woman had been killed?' 'Very much,' he replied, but – and here he tossed back his blond curls – 'that was the pity of war, wasn't it, that innocents got killed. Though it could be argued,' he added, 'that anyone content to live under a Communist dictatorship wasn't really innocent.' Then, while in socialist living-rooms throughout Scotland went up the anguished cry 'The bastard!' he laughed boyishly and began to talk of the places in America where he was going to speak. One was Hollywood. He mentioned the names of some actresses he hoped to meet. The verdict in Lunderston, where there were few socialist living-rooms, was that he had done quite well, but then a man who had faced machine-guns was not going to quail before a few questions asked by a dishy young woman in a red, yellow, and black blouse.

Councillor Rankin could not bear to watch. As soon as Hilderson appeared on the screen he rushed to his bedroom, from where he kept shouting, 'Is he still on?' His wife kept shouting back, rather impatiently, that he was. The interview lasted no more than three minutes, which was as well, for every second of it was torture to the Councillor. At last his wife cried, 'It's finished. You can come ben now.' He found that the champion of freedom had been replaced by a dour trade unionist defending his members who were on strike, hardly an improvement, for one of Councillor Rankin's strongest beliefs was that all strikes should be banned by law.

Annie knew what would give him most pain, and at once

said it, 'We've got to admit he's a very good-looking man. I can see why Sadie fancied him. I wouldn't be surprised if he became a film star himself.'

'There was a time when you wanted him to be libbed. I hope Sadie didn't see him.'

Three weeks ago Sadie had had her sixth child. If she had been watching Hilderson it was probably while giving suck.

'If I was younger I could fancy him myself. Not that I'm all that old. I'm not fifty yet but you treat me as if I was seventy. I read in the *Woman's World* about couples of over eighty still making love. When was the last time we did?'

He was appalled by her frivolity while serious matters waited to be discussed. 'I didn't mark it on the calendar.'

'I did. It was January fourth, six months ago. I'd to beg you, God help me. I have to say that I've had more pleasure in sucking a sweetie, and it didn't last half as long.'

Casting up in this matter of marital love-making was painful and demeaning to him, so he refrained. He could have said it was Annie who had wanted the change to single beds, and it was she, not he, who put cream on her face every night, who wore a flannel nightgown down to her ankles, and who went to bed with steel curlers in her hair.

'I want to talk seriously, Annie.'

'Isn't our love-life a serious subject?'

'About wee John and Hilderson. I'm wondering if I should try and arrange a meeting between them. After all, he *is* the boy's father.'

'He's never shown any interest.'

'This could be the last chance for them to meet. When wee John grows up and learns that we let the chance go by he might not forgive us. You never know, Hilderson might be pleased and grateful, as he ought to be. What man wouldn't be proud of having a son like wee John? He might even want to take him with him to America. Mind you, I don't think we would allow that.'

'I thought I was the romantic one of the family, Jack.'

'You're not a man, Annie. You don't understand a man's feelings about having a son.'

'I understand that you've always held it against me that we never had one.'

'That's nonsense.' But it wasn't really.

'You think of wee John as if he was your son, not your grandson. I'm surprised you'd let Hilderson have him.'

He was surprised himself; he hadn't thought of it in that way. 'For the boy's sake, Annie, should I make the attempt at least?'

'I'm not sure, Jack. It could be a mistake. You'd have to ask Sadie's permission. And Rab's too. He's the boy's legal guardian.'

'All right. I'll ask them.'

Next morning big Bella, one of his assistants in the shop, a jocular middle-aged spinster, remarked that it was a pity they couldn't have Hilderson on television every night, look how good it was for business. Women who usually bought their greengroceries from rival establishments came in, as if hoping to see the blond hero behind the counter. Bella had a figure like two sackfuls of potatoes, but Jack was always as chivalrous towards her as if she was as shapely as Raquel Welsh. Now he was tempted to be rude, especially when she whispered with a wink that she had spent all last night lamenting that Hilderson wasn't in bed beside her. Apples, from South Africa, were close-by, rosy-red; but Bella showed not a blush. Women, he thought, would never be the equals of men, as long as they let themselves be deceived by appearances.

He telephoned Sadie. 'I feel we owe it to wee John.'

She sounded defeated. 'I didn't see him on television. How did he look?'

'I didn't see him either.'

'Did Mum see him?'

'Yes.' Was Annie right? Had he made a mistake?

'What did she think?'

He couldn't lie. 'She thought he was as good-looking as ever.'

That started Sadie weeping.

'Look, Sadie love, I'm sorry. I shouldn't have bothered you.'

'No, Dad, it's all right. Wee John's his son. He should get a chance to see him, if he wants to. Wee John's always asking about him.'

'You don't mind then if I go up to Goatfell House and put it to him?'

'No.'

'What about Rab? Would he mind?'

'It's got nothing to do with him.'

He let that pass.

'If you see him, Dad, give him my love.'

Like hell I will, he cried within. Outwardly he said: 'I'll be friendly if he is.'

She was weeping louder now.

I should take a gun with me, he thought, and shoot the treacherous bastard.

In the evening Jack drove up the hill to Mrs Hilderson's, dressed as if for church or a funeral or a council meeting. The sun sparkled on the Firth. In the mountains of Arran the Warrior slept, after, so local legend had it, conquering all the evil in the world. It was easy to believe it that evening of blue skies, with roses blooming in every garden and birds singing blithely.

He had heard that Mrs Hilderson had allowed her property

20

to run down, not because she lacked the means to keep it in good order, but because she had lost heart. The iron gates were rusty, the driveway full of potholes and weeds, the rhododendrons overgrown, and the big house itself, with all its blinds down, dismal-looking, even in the bright sunshine. Jack might have thought that there was no one living there if it hadn't been for a car at the front door, a red Vauxhall Cavalier. He saw from a sticker that it belonged to a Glasgow firm of car hirers. It must be Hilderson's.

Why was it, just when he needed all the power of forgiveness that he was capable of, that he found himself shaking with rage as he thought of the man who had so callously wronged his daughter. For God's sake, Jack, he told himself, you've come to make peace with Hilderson and offer him God's greatest gift, a son, not a puling infant either but a splendid little lad of eleven. Even if he rejects your offer, though it's inconceivable that he will, it's up to you, as a man who believes in God, to act calmly and without bitterness. You will simply tell him sorrowfully and with dignity that the loss is his, though he might not realise it until he was old and it was too late. 'Don't lose your temper, Jack,' Annie had said. She should have known that he never lost his temper. Sometimes he might be more passionate than the occasion called for, but that was because he cared so much for truth and justice. Speaking to Hilderson, and also to Mrs Hilderson if she deigned to show her face, he would subdue his passion and speak humbly, whatever provocations were heaped on him.

With a hand smelling of apples he banged the big knocker in the shape of a lion's head. It should have been shining brass but was green with verdigris.

As he waited he looked down on Lunderston, his native town, which as a councillor it was his duty to look after and protect. Its public lavatories, open now because it was

21

summer, would not be closed again this winter, as they had been last winter, he would see to that. Yonder were those in the West Bay, being well patronised as he could see. Yonder those on Kirk Brae. Yonder those in the gardens behind the supermarket. Only one who loved the town and knew it well could have picked them out. Yonder too was Brisbane Avenue, with its rows of red-roofed bungalows, his was one of those facing the football field. Annie would be sitting in it now, reading the Barbara Cartland romance she had bought that afternoon. Or maybe she would be on the telephone to Sadie, talking about his mission to Hilderson. She had promised to say nothing until he returned with his report, but she was impatient, like most women. In his experience as a councillor and greengrocer it was women who were always complaining, about holes in the pavements or potatoes with rotten insides, and they weren't willing to wait for a decent interval to let things be remedied. They wanted miracles of quickness. Men knew the difficulties and made allowances.

The door opened at last and he was looking at the only man he had ever hated. Though coarser than he had been at sixteen Hilderson was still damnably handsome and carefree. He was wearing tan slacks, red shirt, cashmere pullover, and dark-red shoes, all of the very best quality. His hair was bleached by the sun. It ought by rights to have been cropped like a convict's and he ought to have been wearing prison clothes.

With a great effort Jack smiled. Hilderson was already smiling, with self-satisfaction. He hadn't recognised Jack as Sadie's father.

'Are you from the local *Herald*?' he asked.

'The local paper is the *Gazette*. I am not a reporter. My name is Councillor Rankin.'

'Well, if you've come to invite me to a civic do it's not on. I'm flying off to the States tomorrow.'

'Tomorrow?'

22

'To London first and then New York.'

'I see. I am not here on behalf of the council, Mr Hilderson. My business is personal and private. Could we step inside?'

'Better not. The house is a bit musty. My mother doesn't keep it aired.' Hilderson was grinning, as if he had just seen the joke, whatever it was. 'Did you say your name's Rankin?'

'I did.'

'Are you a greengrocer?'

'I am.'

'Susie's dad?'

'My daughter's name is Sadie.'

'Sure, Sadie. How is she? I've heard she's done well for herself, married a farmer and has a dozen kids.'

'She has six. One of them is yours.'

'Come off it, Councillor. You're not going to pin that on me.'

As if it was a bloody medal, thought Jack. He heard and saw seagulls. He imagined they were vultures, ready to devour a corpse. It was as well he hadn't brought a gun.

'If you recall, Mr Hilderson, you left Lunderston suddenly about eleven years ago because you had got my daughter pregnant.'

'Councillor, it I'd pleaded guilty to all the times I've been accused of that I'd be the father of a tribe, not all of them the same colour.'

'The marriage was arranged. You sneaked off. It was not the act of an honourable man.'

'I was only a boy, Councillor, and wasn't there some doubt as to who the father was?'

More than ever the gulls sounded like vultures. 'That is an insulting observation, Mr Hilderson. There was no doubt. Your own mother accepted your responsibility. She has been contributing towards the child's upkeep.'

'My mother's a bit peculiar.'

'The boy happens to be your image.'

'When people are looking for resemblances they can always see them. They see them in dogs even.'

Jack might have struck him then, though it would have been difficult, Hilderson being much taller and standing on a step, but they were joined by Mrs Hilderson walking with the help of a stick. Jack was amazed to see that her hair was snow-white, though she was hardly any older than himself. She did look peculiar. Judging from the faraway look in her eyes she was away with the fairies, as they said in Lunderston. She didn't smell fresh either.

'What is it, Gary?' She asked. 'Who is this person?'

'I'm Councillor Rankin,' said that person. 'Sadie's father. I've come to ask your son if he would like to meet his son, towards whose keep you have been contributing for the past eleven years. It may be his sense of humour or it could be that his recent experiences have deranged him, but he has denied paternity.'

'Does it matter,' she asked contemptuously, 'who your father is?'

She did not wait for an answer, but if she had waited an hour or all night or all year Jack, flabbergasted, could not have given her one. *Did* it really matter? Whether your father was the murderer hanged for his crime or the judge who had sentenced him you were yourself, you couldn't be blamed for anything you hadn't done yourself. Men who had run the concentration camps during the War had sons and daughters who in Germany today were respectable citizens.

These thoughts were whirling in Jack's mind as Hilderson, laughing, stepped inside and shut the door. Gazing at the green lion Jack wondered where he was. Then he turned to the spires of Lunderston or of heaven? Annie would scold him for having made a mess of his mission, Sadie would weep, and

24

wee John would be sorely disappointed. Nevertheless he felt that he had succeeded in a way that he could never explain to anyone. He had been let into a secret.

No one would notice any difference in him. Annie would criticise and Bella make fun. He would still be called a wee Fascist. At council meetings his proposals would still be rejected as being far-fetched and impracticable. Behind his back people would still laugh at him, the diminutive greengrocer with the big ideas. All that was true, but he would find it easier to forgive them, because he knew now that they were all, every single one of them, including Communists and shoplifters, special and unique.

It probably would not last, this inspiration, old habits of thought and prejudices would blot it out, but echoes would be with him for the rest of his life.

The Provost and the Queen

FOR HUNDREDS OF YEARS before the recent lamentable restructuring of local government in the interests of the false gods efficiency and economy Lunderston, like all the burghs in Scotland, had its own town council and its own provost. In those homelier days you saw a councillor in the street every day and could have it out with him man-to-man concerning any grievance you might have had or any municipal improvement you were keen to advocate. It was a family affair. In these so-called efficient and economical times of district councils that meet in distant places decisions regarding your own town are taken by a gaggle of councillors from other towns, men and women you've never set eyes on. It was strangers like these who not long ago voted to close Lunderston's public lavatories during the off-season, in spite of the protests of the two Lunderston councillors who pointed out that their town being by the sea suffered from chilly winds in winter and had a large proportion of elderly citizens with weak bladders.

There was the Provost's chain of office, worn round his neck at all council functions. In Lunderston's case it had been more brass than gold but kept well polished it had a ducal look. More venerable than the chain and more historical was the Lunderston Missal, as it was called, the Toon's Ain Buik, about the size of a family Bible, in which were inscribed the signatures of famous people who had visited the town; among them were Mary, Queen of Scots, and the present monarch Queen Elizabeth. Its batters were of red leather faded and scuffed with age. Engraved on the front was the town's emblem, a seagull with in its beak a fish that had in its mouth a smaller fish; and the town's motto, found in documents going back to the time of Robert the Bruce, 'Naething Wasted.' It was kept in a glass case in the burgh chambers, on a piece of red velvet. It was said that there had also been a quill pen, the one used by Mary Stuart, but this had got lost or stolen or perhaps had just crumbled with age.

The last provost but two before the dissolution of the office was John Golspie, the most notorious in the town's history, guilty of what in many townspeople's opinion was worse than rape or murder. He arrived in the town one cold December, a hulking glowering young man, wearing a thick black coat with a fur collar, and carrying a bag stuffed with money. So the story went anyway. How he got it and where he had come from were never established. Even then when he was not yet thirty he was not a man to pester with inconvenient questions. Big, over six feet, and heavy, over fourteen stones, he had a low brow and coarse red face, hands like a navvy's, and a voice that could be heard, it was claimed, from within the council chambers by folk strolling on the promenade half a mile away.

At first Big Jock, as he soon came to be called, lived in a two-roomed cottage in the slum district known as the Vennel. There, so slyly that it was some time before people were aware of what he was up to, he carried on his business. He bought up dilapidated tenements cheaply, refurbished them at little cost, and then rented them at high rents. He also snapped up plots of vacant land all over the town, at that time, just after the War, going for low prices to anyone with ready cash. As a sideline he lent money to carefully chosen clients, at scandalous rates of interest.

Even in those early days he had his heart set on being Provost, not because of the honour or because he was eager to serve the community, but because he wanted to be top man. When he first put himself up as a candidate for the council he had no difficulty in finding the required number of sponsors from among those in his financial clutches, but at the election, which of course was by secret ballot, the people of the ward he had chosen showed what they thought of him by giving him 51 votes out of a total of 875. One of the questions put to him by hecklers was: 'During the War, Mr Golspie, were you ever in uniform?' Not a bit fashed, he replied that unfortunately he had been rejected on medical grounds, but he had served his country in other capacities; he refused to say what these were. Then, with a brazenness not commonly found among petitioners for votes, he challenged his baiters to stand up and tell what heroic exploits *they* had won their VCs for. Thus it was learned that there was a new kind of politician active in the town, one who did not hesitate to show his contempt for those whose votes he was seeking. At that time all candidates stood as Independents, though they were really Tories, some more reactionary than others. Big Jock described himself as a free-thinking, honest-speaking individualist. 'I'm a bigger man physically, and in any other way you like to mention, than any other man in this town. I'm going to be the most famous Provost you ever had. What I'll do I'll do for myself, let me be frank about that, but the town will benefit too. Just you wait.'

Well, they waited, for nearly twenty years, and sure enough he did become Provost. He had got himself elected councillor for the Ardgartan Ward which included within its boundaries the fine big villas along the East Bay. In the pubs where the poorer sort drank no one was surprised that Big Jock had got the well-to-do to elect him. Though they deplored his vulgarity they had decided that he was their man. They knew that he was a crook, but their kind of crook, who could be depended on to protect their privileges.

Though it would have been hard to find anyone who had a good word for him Big Jock became the most powerful man in town. He was re-elected councillor with bigger and bigger majorities, and in due course the two lamp-posts, with the town's coat-of-arms painted on the glass, appeared in the street outside his house, by which it was made known to all the world that therein dwelled the Provost of Lunderston.

It was not of course the two-roomed cottage with the outside toilet, in the Vennel; that area had long since been demolished. It was one of the villas in the East Bay. They were large and built of the same grey stone as churches, solid, dignified, and commanding respect. Their owners had allowed themselves some individuality in the colour with which the woodwork was painted, but all had agreed, without ever discussing it, that a discreet colour like dark-blue or dark-green would be appropriate. The stone was left untouched. The result was a row of houses of quiet distinction. Not only were their owners proud of them; so was the whole town.

Big Jock had been Provost only three weeks when he had his villa painted a bright pink, front, back, gables, and chimneys. He bought two life-size china lions – God knew from where – to be placed on either side of his front door. These too he had painted pink, with their noses and the tips of their tails golden.

The town was aghast. Why had he done it? There were many conjectures.

It was to affront his neighbours. They voted for him but they didn't invite him to their homes, nor did they accept invitations to his.

It was to make it known to passengers on planes coming

down to land at Prestwick a few miles away, and to passing yachtsmen on the Firth, that there lived Big Jock Golspie, Provost of Lunderston.

He had been given the paint free. Like all money-lenders he was tight-fisted.

So far as anybody knew he had never been to sunny lands like Italy and Spain where houses were brightly painted, but perhaps he had seen them in pictures.

He really thought he was brightening up the East Bay, which to a person of his crude taste might seem rather drab.

It was while they were joking among themselves, grimly, about his pink house, that the townsfolk realised as never before how solitary Big Jock was. He had no friends or confidants who could be consulted as to his motive, or who could have advised him against such a monstrosity of bad taste. He neither smoked nor drank, out of meanness many people thought, but it could have been principle of some kind, though he went to church only as Provost, wearing his chain, never as himself. He had never married; indeed, so far as was known, he had never had a woman friend. That he preferred celibacy was his business and only rude boozers in the pubs were ribald about it, but if he had had a wife or even a mistress, she would surely have prevented him from making so ghastly a mistake, unless of course she had the same vulgar taste as himself, which wasn't unlikely, for he wouldn't have chosen any other kind of woman.

But what emphasised his loneliness most of all was that there wasn't one person in the whole of Lunderston who felt close enough to him or liked him well enough to ask: For God's sake, Jock, why pink? He seemed to have no relatives. What were his hobbies, how did he pass his private hours, what possessions gave him most pleasure, what secret regrets did he have? No one knew.

*   *   *

Glowering at the top of the table, with his fists pounding it like hammers and his roars heard in the street outside, Big Jock had all his councillors cowed. They complained to their wives that he turned up at the meetings not just with the chain round his neck but dressed in striped breeks, black jacket, and stiff white collar, as if he was Prime Minister, while the rest of them looked so common, in lounge suits and pullovers. They had thought of wearing formal dress themselves in retaliation but the absurdity of it and the cost of it deterred them.

Though among the citizens in general he was far from popular he had nevertheless won the reputation of getting things done, in contrast to the fushionlessness of the rest of the council. If tinkers parked their van too near your hotel, to the annoyance of your guests, it was no use your protesting to the police, they just mumbled that they had been given orders not to harass the travelling people. What you did then, whether or not you lived in Big Jock's ward, was lift the telephone and ask his help. Within a couple of hours the police would arrive in force and the nuisances would be moved on. Similarly if a new washer was wanted on a tap in your council house and you had complained to the Clerk of Works several times without his bothering to do anything about it, you just let Big Jock know and there were two workmen, let alone one, at your door within an hour. He did it by the force of his physical presence, for as he got older he got more massive, and by the volume of his voice, but there had to be something else. He had no doubt himself what it was; he was a big man among little men. If you had said a pike among minnows he would have nodded.

But for his insulting behaviour towards the Queen his obituary, when it came to be written, would have had to be grudgingly laudatory, but even the few republicans in the town thought he disgraced himself then beyond recovery. Not, to be fair, that he ever admitted that he had done anything wrong, and he claimed to have witnesses who would have spoken in his defence, the Queen herself and Prince Philip.

During his term of office as Provost the building of the new conference hall was begun and completed. It had been proposed years before but he could certainly claim credit for bringing it about. Whether or not he had insisted on alterations to the architect's plans, as was alleged, the result was, alas, a dreary, unlikeable building inside and out. What ought to have been an embellishment to the town was an eyesore. Appalled and disappointed, the ratepayers' only consolation was that it had cost a great deal of money. No one could say that it had been ruined by cheapness.

Big Jock himself thought it magnificent, so much so that only one person in the land was fit to declare it open. He meant the Queen. For God's sake, Jock, muttered the councillors, in embarrassment, you can't expect Her Majesty to find the time to come to Lunderston to open a mere conference hall. They shuddered as they thought what Prince Philip, a forthright critic, would say about the building. Big Jock scowled but was not dissuaded. He went personally to discuss it with the Lord Lieutenant, who liked the idea. They were lucky. The Queen's advisers, looking at Lunderston on the map and finding it close to seditious and republican Glasgow, must have seen the propaganda value in her paying it a visit. The royal yatch could anchor off Lunderston on its way up round Pentland to Aberdeen, and the Queen could disembark for an hour or so to declare open the hall or whatever it was, with television cameras present, and hundreds of school children supplied with little Union Jacks. In such a douce and loyal town there would be no danger of loutish demonstrators. Therefore, in due course, an important-looking letter came from Buckingham Palace saying that Her Majesty had graciously consented. Big Jock, remover of tinkers' vans and mender of leaky taps, had brought off the supreme triumph of his life.

When he announced it to his councillors they were thunder-struck. Men who despised him babbled apologies. Their fear of Prince Philip's ridicule was forgotten. No one actually knelt down and kissed Big Jock's shoes but their submission was just as abject as if they had. They havered among themselves that they ought to do something to show not just their appreciation of his bringing upon the burgh the greatest honour in its history – the visit of Mary, Queen of Scots, was too far distant for comparison – but also their contrition at having so meanly underestimated him. One even suggested having a statue of him erected in front of the town hall; after all, he'd pay for it himself.

When it was made public in the *Lunderston Gazette* that the Queen was going to open the new Conference Hall everybody was astonished and delighted. It did not need the editor to remind them that this wonderful honour to the town had been achieved by their Provost, Mr John Golspie. They all knew it. Big Jock might be a vulgar, arrogant, ignorant brute, but he could get things done. Old ladies stopped him in the street and congratulated him. Letters to the *Gazette* sternly reminded the townspeople that they had not in the past shown sufficient gratitude to Mr Golspie for all his endeavours on their behalf. This must be remedied forthwith. No doubt the Queen would award him an OBE, but he must also be made a freeman of the town. When his term of office as Provost expired he must, as a special privilege, be permitted to keep the two lamp-posts outside his house; the custom being to take one away, to distinguish between present and past provosts. There were some people, said one letter, who had condemned Mr Golspie's painting of his house pink. They should at once withdraw that criticism. Mr

Golspie deserved that his house be a vivid landmark. Indeed, once he was no longer with us, ought not the burgh to buy the house and so ensure that it remained gloriously pink?

So high was his standing in the town that there were some people, that day in June, who gave Big Jock the credit for the blue skies and warm sunshine, especially as the day before had been overcast and rainy. In his pink mansion what magic had he evoked? When the *Britannia* came sailing round Cumbrae and anchored off Lunderston pier, sounding its siren in salutation, there was such a brightness in the air, such a purity and clarity, that everything seemed newly created for the occasion, from the pebbles on the beach to the hills of Arran in the distance. Few people could remember so splendid a day. There were only two words to describe it, royal and heavenly. Some there thought, secretly, with catches of their breaths, as they saw the Queen waving to the children, that she was not just greeting them, she was blessing them too. She was dressed in blue, the Madonna's colour, and had pearls round her neck.

As she stepped on to the pier, which was covered with red carpet, she was bowed to first by the Lord Lieutenant with his feathered hat and then by the Provost representing the town, with his gray lum hat in his hand and his chain of office glinting in the sun. His citizens saw with pride how, knowing his place, he stood respectfully back. Prince Philip, in naval uniform, chatted to him amiably, though it must have been difficult for them to hear each other, such a din was being made by the pipe band, the seagulls, and the cheering children.

The official party, with the Provost and the Lord Lieutenant accompanying the royal couple, was driven in Jimmy Paterson's funereal Rolls Royces, through streets crammed with spectators, to the conference hall three hundred yards away.

34

The ceremony of unveiling the plaque and declaring the hall open was to be followed by a brief tour of the building, during which the Queen was to sign the Lunderston Missal. All the councillors and town officials and their wives were in attendance. Afterwards they were to be ferried out to the royal yatch for afternoon tea. Promptly at four they would be ferried back, so that Her Majesty would be able to continue her voyage towards the Hebrides. Nervous, for they had never before been in such exalted company, the councillors kept looking to their Provost for example and courage.

Afterwards accounts differed as to how he had done it. The councillors and town officials were keyed up and there was a screen of equerries, ladies-in-waiting, and bodyguards between them and the royal visitors, but the account generally accepted was that at one point in the tour of the hall, with the Provost acting as her guide, he produced a large handsome album with red leather covers and invited the Queen to sign it. (It was jaloused that he must have had it planked in readiness, with the connivance of some workman.) In any case the Queen, though surprised, for she probably expected a little more ceremony, signed it with the gold fountain pen that the Provost handed her. She was even more surprised when, minutes later, in the room specially prepared, she was asked to sign again, this time in the authentic book. It appeared that she said something to the Provost, perhaps reminding him that she had already signed. He made some reply, whereupon, with a glance at Prince Philip and a smile to herself, she signed. Then, minutes later, up to time, they were all out of the building and on their way to the pier. The deed of shame had been done and there was its perpetrator, looking mightily pleased with himself.

According to Councillors Grant and Donaldson they were approached on the yacht by Prince Philip, who seemed half-indignant and half-amused. Could they tell him what the big fellow with the top hat and red face had been up to, with the two town Missals? Surely it was unusual to have two. Was it an insurance against one of them being devoured by mice or rotted with damp? Or had one of them belonged to the big chap himself? If so then he had a damned cheek. Did they agree or were they all in it? Miserably but earnestly they assured him that it was all the Provost's doing. No one had known that he was going to do it. An explanation would be demanded.

They had to admit afterwards that the Prince had not seemed all that offended and had given the impression that he and the Queen when they were alone would enjoy a laugh at the extraordinary impudence of the Provost of Lunderston.

No one in the town laughed. They were all shocked and shamed.

Behind the Provost's back the councillors sought the advice of the town clerk, who was a lawyer. Could the Provost be charged with degrading his office? There was no such offence. Could he be dismissed, with ignominy, before his term was expired? It wouldn't be easy, for he would fight them all the way up to the Court of Session. Well, couldn't a vote of censure be passed, after which surely he wouldn't have the effrontery to remain, not only in the Provost's chair but in the town itself? Such a vote was up to the council, said the town clerk, but he sounded as if he didn't think they had the necessary resolution. In any case if the Provost chose to ignore it, as he doubtless would, that would be the end of it. The councillors were incensed. They could name countries which had found it easier to get rid of kings or presidents.

The meeting took place at which the Provost was to be censured and asked to resign. The public gallery was full. People had queued for hours to get in. Others waited out in the street, in the rain. Every councillor was present, even one who had risen from his death bed; he died three days later.

36

One of the bailies put the charge and the other called upon the Provost to make some amends by apologising to the town and then leaving it for good. 'Russia's the place for you,' one councillor muttered. Other councillors stood up and spoke, supporting the motion. Big Jock sat in silence, sucking peppermints, with his big fists resting on the table. Now and then he rifted. It was noticed how white hair that made other men look venerable made him look villainous. They were disgusted with themselves for having elected as their Provost such a coarse brute. They ought to have known that he would disgrace them. It broke their hearts to see him wearing the chain.

When they had had their say they waited for him to respond. If he had broken down and wept and flung himself upon their mercy they would have been embarrassed and uncertain, for some of them had known him for over thirty years and like themselves he was an old man. If he had committed murder and was about to be hanged they might for auld lang syne's sake have pitied him in the condemned cell and shaken his hand; but what he had done was worse than murder, though they couldn't have said exactly what it was.

At last he spoke or rather growled, 'I don't know what all the fuss is about. What happened was between me and Her Majesty. She didn't object, so why should you? No man in this room or in this town honours her more than me, but, dammit, she's not God Almighty. That's all I'm going to say on the subject.'

And in spite of their clamour he kept his word.

Of course it wasn't enough. In fact he had added to the insult to the Queen by saying she wasn't God Almighty. They hadn't needed the big clown to tell them that. They had all been to school. They knew that her ancestors Jamie the Saxt and Charles had got into trouble by claiming divine right; the latter had had his head chopped off. All that had been fought

over and settled long ago. In the Queen's presence people did
humble themselves more than they did before the Moderator
of the Church of Scotland or the Archbishop of Canterbury
(though not more than Catholics did before the Pope) but
that was because she represented the grandeur and majesty
of the State, not because they took her for God. They knew
all that, but they shouldn't be made to say it openly because
a big ignoramus had been discourteous and disrespectful, if
not quite blasphemous.

No one was sorry for him. Afterwards as he walked down
the main street people stepped into the gutter so as not
to rub shoulders with him. Many for whom he had done
favours crossed the street to avoid him. One old lady, Mrs
McDougall, who lived in an East Bay villa, stopped him once
but it was to slap his face. Those who saw it said that he just
glowered and strode on. At the next election he did not
put himself forward as a candidate. One of the lamp-posts
outside his house was removed with all haste. In retaliation,
it was thought, he had his house repainted, a brighter pink
than before.

When he died, aged seventy-five, the general opinion,
privately whispered, was good riddance. In his obituary in the
Gazette the episode of the fraudulently obtained autograph
was mentioned. 'It was the most curious episode in a curious
man's career. No one knew why he did it. He offered no
explanation. For forty years he was one of the most familiar
figures in the town and yet no one ever knew him.'

After the abolition of the town council the Lunderston
Missal went missing. It happened at a time of acrimonious
argument as to its rightful owners, whether the burgh, which
really was no longer a burgh but simply a part of the district,
or the District Council. If, muttered the townspeople, some
loyal Lunderstonian had purloined it to save it from falling
into the hands of outsiders, and if he was preserving it till

the day that Lunderston would be a burgh again, running its own affairs, then good luck to him.

Ironically, among the relics of the town later gathered into a kind of museum in the old burgh hall, the most revered was Provost Golspie's album, containing the Queen's signature.

Don't You Agree, Baby?

WHEN IT READS ABOUT racial riots in English cities and sees scenes of violence and hatred on television screens Lunderston congratulates itself on being free from that particular virulence, though it honestly admits that it does not have the same strains and provocations as the white citizens of Birmingham for instance. The only coloured intruders it has to contend with are the Khans from North India who own a restaurant and discotheque, the Chungs from Hong Kong who also own a restaurant, and some black Americans from the nearby air base. These last once caused a commotion in the town, smashing shop windows and alarming the citizenry, but drunkenness was to blame and also jealousy over some good-for-nothing local girls who favoured the blacks because of their money and also, it was whispered, their superior virility. But the windows had been quickly repaired, compensation paid, the culprits punished by their own authorities, and an apology received, not from the President it was true but from an officer of high rank, so the episode was soon forgiven if not forgotten and goodwill restored. As for the Indians and Chinese there might be grumbles about their being more prosperous than native restaurateurs but most people were prepared to give them credit for showing more enterprise and being willing to work much longer hours.

Don't You Agree, Baby?

If you stopped Lunderstonians in the street and asked if it made any difference to them what a person's colour of skin was they would, hand on heart, deny it. Their denials would be sincere even if not quite truthful.

The Rev. Mr Colin McLeish had been minister of the Scottish Episcopal church in Lunderston for over thirty years. His congregation was never more than thirty but the church and rectory, situated by a burn on the outskirts of the town, were charming ivy-covered edifices, so that he had never any ambition to seek promotion and move to busier less pleasant pastures. His only child Ian was born in the rectory and his wife died in it, the one event preceding the other by only two years. Educated at Lunderston Primary, Lunderston Academy, and the Scottish Episcopal College in Glasgow, young Ian became a minister like his father and grandfather before him. Unlike them, as soon as he was ordained, he went off to be assistant to an Anglican bishop in the South of India. There in Travancore he made himself useful, often conducting services in a church from whose front steps could be seen both the Arabian Sea and the Gulf of Bengal. He wrote home to say that there was not a single white person in the congregation.

This adventurous streak in Ian surprised some of his father's flock who remembered him as a solemn stout young man with big ears and a squeaky voice. They were still more surprised when they learned that he was to marry the Bishop's youngest daughter. He enclosed a black-and-white photograph of the young lady who could be seen to have fine teeth and dark eyes almost coquettish with their frank gaze. Because of the wrong positioning of the photographer, which caused the light to be badly dispersed, her face looked quite fair but her shoulder, bare because she was wearing a saree, seemed quite dark. Old Mr McLeish was not able to attend the wedding, being too frail to undertake so long a journey but he sent his blessing

41

and also, to the bride, rings that had belonged to his wife, for he, and others, had gathered from the photograph that his future daughter-in-law was fond of jewellery; rather odd, some of his parishioners thought, in a bishop's daughter. Her name was Mary Magdalene but it seemed she preferred to be called Kamala.

Thanks to the efforts of a parishioner the photograph appeared in the *Gazette* so that it was scrutinised and commented on in many Lunderston households. It was generally known that the Tamils of South India were pretty dark but in this rather smudgy picture the degree of negritude of Ian's wife-to-be was doubtful. Was she as dark as her shoulder or as fair as her face? What was clear enough was that she had a vivacious smile and lively eyes. Some who remembered Ian as dull and humourless wondered that he should have won the heart of such a delightful girl.

About two years after his son's marriage, in the month of June when the roses were in bloom in all the gardens, old Mr McLeish became seriously ill. According to the doctor he would not last much longer. So it was decided to send an urgent message to Ian to come home so that he could be reunited with his father before the end. It was also hoped, though not yet mentioned, that he would stay and take his father's place.

Two elders, Mr Blair and Mr Dyce, were deputed to go to Glasgow airport to meet the young couple who had flown from Madras to Delhi, then to London, and on to Glasgow, a journey to tax a healthy person let alone a woman of twenty with child. Therefore as they waited behind the barrier in the Arrivals Hall they were expecting to find her worn-out and paler than usual, whatever her usual happened to be. It was with consternation and other emotions they were careful never to analyse or talk about afterwards even to their wives, that they saw by Ian's side a small young woman in a bright red saree that accentuated if indeed anything could have the sheer blackness of her face. Tar? Soot? Boot polish? Ebony? Coal? The Earl of Hell's waistcoat? None of these was black enough. Neither Mr Blair nor Mr Dyce was a stupid or ignorant man. They knew that the Lord for His own good reasons had seen fit to give to various peoples throughout the world shades of darkness in their complexions and it would have been as unfair to find fault with them as it would have been to praise a polar bear for being white. None the less each of them thought, independently, that Mrs McLeish, even if she should turn out to have angelic qualities, would never do in Lunderston.

Evidently she loved colour despite her skin's total lack of it. Her toenails and lips were red like her saree, on her ears were white blobs of coral, and in her hair a pink flower now wilted.

It did not help them to find the right response and show it on their faces that Ian himself was bald, fat, and flushed. His jacket and trousers were black and lustrous and he wore a white dickey. His hand was clammy but that could have been because of the heat of Travancore. Shaking Mrs McLeish's, Mr Dyce noticed how pink were the tips of her fingers and her palm.

Still more disconcerting was McLeish's addressing of his wife as Baby. Afterwards they were to learn that this was the Bishop's pet name for his youngest daughter which her husband had copied, but at the airport Mr Blair and Mr Dyce were reminded ludicrously of tough American film stars like the late Humphrey Bogart. McLeish said it pompously, as indeed he said everything else.

Never had Mr Blair's Volvo looked so white as he approached it in the car-park and all the other cars round it dazzled with their variety of colour, though earlier that day he had hardly noticed them.

During the journey to Lunderston they talked sadly about Ian's father. Mr Dyce thought of the old man waiting to greet his daughter-in-law. Expecting some kind of shining angel, for according to his housekeeper Mrs MacPherson his delirious murmurings could be so interpreted, what would be the effect on him of looking up and seeing a face that, though angelically sweet, was none the less as black as the Devil? For old Mr McLeish believed in the Devil, not just as an idea representing evil but as a physical presence. He had persisted in exorcising houses which to tell the truth had been troubled by nothing worse than mice, sighing draughts, or mischievous teenagers.

McLeish, the returned exile, gazed out at the landscapes of home. 'After Travancore it all seems so drab. Does it not, Baby?'

'You will not sweat so much here, Ian.'

'Perspire is the word, Baby. But neither is ladylike.'

Did Mr Blair in the rear mirror see her wink? Did Mr Dyce hear her chuckle?

'We've all been hoping, Mr McLeish,' said Mr Blair, recklessly, 'that you might stay and deputise for your father and perhaps eventually take his place.'

'It has been on my mind, Mr Blair. I have discussed it with the Bishop. He has graciously said if I so decide he would release me although there is still a great deal of work for me to do yonder. The Catholics have been making encroachments. We have been losing members. I was in the midst of a campaign of recruitment when the news came of my father.'

'You'd have no trouble with Catholics in Lunderston,' said Mr Dyce. 'There's not much poaching of souls there.'

'I am not unaware that my primary duty might lie among my own people. There are those who accuse us missionaries of going far afield to win souls for Christ when there are plenty of souls at home to be won.'

'Lunderston has its share of heathens all right,' said Mr Dyce.

'Would a display of fervour bring them into the fold? Who knows?'

'Ian is famous for fervour,' said Mrs McLeish, whether humorously or naively Mr Blair and Mr Dyce could not be sure.

'The Bishop has very kindly praised my evangelical gifts,' said McLeish.

Mr Blair and Mr Dyce exchanged a quick anxious glance. The last thing the Holy Trinity congregation needed or wanted was a fat pompous sweaty evangelical minister. His father's eccentricities, such as exorcising houses or pausing in a sermon to identify the bird singing outside, had been tolerable but a ranter in the pulpit was not to be borne. People in Lunderston joined the Episcopals for peace and quiet.

They descended the steep brae into the town. They saw the tall spire of St Cuthbert's.

'Does Mr Henderson still occupy its pulpit?' asked McLeish.

'He does,' replied Mr Blair. 'He's been there for thirty years.'

'If I remember correctly he is not evangelical.'

'That's not his style,' said Mr Dyce.

'As a consequence, I suppose,' said McLeish, with a pompous sigh, 'faith among his flock has become lukewarm.'

'I wouldn't call it burning hot,' said Mr Blair.

They drove along the main street.

'Are White's strawberry tarts still as delicious?' asked McLeish, licking his lips. 'I have often missed them.'

They were passing the baker's shop.

'I don't suppose we could stop and buy some? No, it is too congested. Please drive on, Mr Blair.'

*   *   *

45

Mrs MacPherson was at the front door of the rectory to welcome them.

McLeish was first out of the car. He looked about him. He heard the burn but could not see it because of the trees. An elm was so close to the house that its furthermost leaves tapped against the roof. 'Some of these trees must be cut down,' he said, 'to let in more sunlight.'

Yet, thought Mr Dyce, as he helped Mrs McLeish out of the car, if ever there was a man with a wife that needed shade it was McLeish. Indeed, she made for it at once.

Led by Mrs MacPherson they crept upstairs in the old wood-panelled, fresh-smelling, flower-bedecked house, where the sun came in through the small windows in big splashes. The old man, Mrs MacPherson had said, would probably be asleep. He slept most of the time.

She went in first to prepare the dying man. He was awake, for they heard her speaking to him: 'Your son Ian and his wife have arrived, Mr McLeish. They are outside. Do you feel able to see them now?'

She came out. 'He wants to see you, Mr McLeish, and you too, Mrs McLeish.'

As Mr Blair and Mr Dyce waited on the small landing they listened to the murmur of voices within the room. Suddenly, freezing their blood, they heard a strange strangled cry, more suited to an infant than a man of seventy-five. As they stared at each other in surmise Mrs McLeish came rushing out, with her hands covering her face, and stumbled down the stairs. She might have fallen if Mr Dyce hadn't caught hold of her. It was to be another lifelong secret that he was amazed to find so soft a shoulder as black as ebony.

'He's gone,' Mrs MacPherson was saying. 'The surprise was too much for him. His heart was hanging by a thread, the doctor said.'

Peeping in, Mr Blair saw Ian on his knees by the bedside.

Even when praying he looked pompous. In the bed his father still looked surprised. But Mr Blair would have used a stronger word.

It did not take the congregation of Holy Trinity long to regret having asked McLeish to take his father's place. His sermons displeased them by being long, obscure, and fervent. Improvements that he advocated for the rectory and church would have cost thousands. His self-praise about his achievements in South India became insufferable, particularly when, as often happened, it was uttered with his mouth full of White's tart or meringue, for not only did he have a sweet tooth he was also greedy. Among his other demands was a new car.

But they might have put up with all that for his old father's sake if only his wife had not been so relentlessly black. They were all profoundly ashamed of themselves but they could not help it. Of course they knew it was not the young woman's fault. If anyone was to blame (leaving God aside) it was her husband. Surely of all the many millions of women in India he could have chosen one not quite so black. On a sideboard in the rectory there was now a coloured photograph of the Bishop's daughters, six in all, including Baby. Two were still unmarried. Though buck-toothed, they seemed several shades lighter than she. Why had he not married one of them?

None of these thoughts was ever uttered aloud. The shame and guilt they felt was too deep.

Everybody wondered, without ever mentioning it, what colour the child would be. Everybody vowed, again without mentioning it, to treat it no differently from any other child.

If Mrs McLeish had been an unpleasant young woman they would have been better able to endure their shame, but on the contrary she was very likeable, in spite of having been pampered by her father the Bishop. She had not a trace of her husband's pomposity and was capable of making gentle fun of it. She had a natural friendliness, like a puppy. Apart from its blackness her face was attractive, with refined features. It was as if blackness had not been nature's original intention. Something had gone wrong. A mistake had been made.

Lunderstonians, outside the Holy Trinity congregation, did their best not to humiliate or embarrass her, but they were not always successful. When she went into a shop the assistants would stop serving and stare. So would the other customers. This lasted only for a few seconds after which the good folk of Lunderston minded their manners and paid the young woman no more overt attention and subjected her to no more rudeness. Had she noticed? She gave no sign, and of course if she had blushed it wouldn't have shown. When it was her turn to be served, though there might have been one or two smiles at her sing-song accent, she was treated like any other customer.

She never complained. Perhaps she did in her letters home, but these she showed to no one, not even her husband.

One evening, about three months after their arrival in Lunderston, Mr and Mrs McLeish were in the rectory sitting-room. She was tapping out simple hymn tunes on the piano and he, with a plateful of chocolate biscuits to fortify him, was looking through last year's financial statement. He was getting ready for the visit of a Scottish bishop in a few days. He did not notice the tears in his wife's eyes.

'Ian,' she said, for the third time.

Again he did not hear her because of the music and the crunching of biscuits.

At last she screamed.

He heard this time. 'Yes, Baby?'

'I want to go home.'

'What was that? What did you say?' Politely he stopped crunching to listen.

'I said I want to go home. I don't want my baby to be born here.'

He smiled. 'But aren't you already home? Are you not my faithful Ruth? Is not my home your home?'

'They treat me here as if I was a freak.'

She stopped playing then and there was silence except for one of the old man's birds singing outside.

His son wondered idly if it was a blackbird or a thrush. 'What did you say, Baby?'

'I said they treat me here as if I was a freak.'

'A freak? Good heavens! In what way a freak?'

'Because I'm so black. They say I frighten their children.'

Again he smiled. 'I've never heard anyone say that. It would be ridiculous. You're no blacker than your father the Bishop.'

'The girls in my school used to jeer at me because I was so black. They were black themselves but I was the blackest of all. My own sisters laughed at me. Look at little Baby, she's as black as charcoal.'

'Do not fret, my dear. All pregnant women have strange fears and fancies. But I am seriously considering if it would be wise for me to stay here. Where is the the challenge? What scope is there for a man of fervour? There are no mountains to be climbed, no deserts to be traversed. I speak figuratively. Life here would be too easy. Don't you agree, Baby?'

The Merry Widow and the Elder

A STRANGER NOTICING HOW NUMEROUS and solid Lunderston's churches were, and how sedate and respectable the worshippers, especially the ladies with their hats and gloves, would never guess that the town was as libertarian in regard to sexual matters as any in Christendom. Two women living together, one of them mannish, or two men, one of them womanish, are called no names, not because the townsfolk are not aware of their peculiar proclivities, but because Lunderston's philosophy has always been that as long as people are discreet and harm no one what they do in private is their business and good luck to them. As for orthodox sex, the sort that most Lunderstonians practise, it is often indulged in for motives more subtle and human than the mere gratification of appetite.

Even before he became a widower at the age of sixty Herbert Howieson had the reputation of being abstemious, austere, and high-minded. After his wife's death, of a prolonged and painful disease, he got worse, in some people's opinion, including his married son's, but according to others, including his married daughter, still better, in that, free now to marry again and well able to afford a wife, he remained celibate and chaste. No other elder of St Cuthbert's took his duties so seriously, whether visiting the sick or standing at the kirk door on Sundays, clad in black.

Some men asked, maliciously, if Herbert at the church door was as unaware as he pretended, how black set off his trim figure and silvery hair, but such scoffers were chided by their wives, who whispered, during the sermon perhaps, that Mr Howieson was to be respected, his mind being on spiritual matters and not physical, by which they meant sexual, like most men's. What about feet? One husband once retorted, chuckling at a joke that his wife refused to appreciate. The point of it was that Herbert owned the best shoe shop in town, selling the most expensive brands. That he would personally attend to some lady from Ailsa Park or the East Bay, well-off areas, showed, if you liked him, a praiseworthy humility, but, if you didn't, a creepiness out of keeping with his reputation for spirituality. Detractors implied that he unnecessarily caressed feet that were shapely and encased in silk, whereas feet that were bumpy with bunions he left to his two assistants Mrs Blacklock who worked for him full-time and Mrs Traquair who worked from ten o'clock to one.

What was the truth about Herbert's sexuality no one knew. Mrs Blackwood, a big plain-faced woman, gave him the benefit of any doubt and pronounced him God-fearing and clean-minded; Mrs Traquair, younger and well-shaped, was not so sure. There were moments when she turned suddenly and there he was staring at her in a very funny way, as if his mind then was more on bottoms and bosoms than on Bibles. He was fond of reading books about Victorian missionaries in Africa. Mrs Traquair once stole a look at one in the back-shop, and was astonished and disturbed to find in it photographs of bearded missionaries, wearing frock coats and top hats, standing beside native women naked except for strings of beads round their middle. However, it wasn't fear of being bludgeoned by a shoe and then raped that caused her to leave his employment. She was offered and accepted a full-time job in a ladies' outfitters.

Mr Howieson put an advertisement in the *Gazette*. Three applicants appeared. Two were swiftly rejected, one being fat and double-chinned, the other skinny and hen-toed. The third was small, red-cheeked, chirpy as a robin, with a neat figure and neat ankles. Mrs Blackwood knew her, as indeed many people in Lunderston did, for Mrs Sellars was well-liked, and thought at first that she had come in as a customer, though it would have surprised her if Mrs Sellars, a widow, with a girl at college, could have afforded Howieson prices. The shoes she was wearing now were cheap and well-worn.

'No, Betty, I'm after that job. Is it still open? Good. Do you think I've got a chance?'

Mrs Blackwood didn't think so. Katie Sellars would be too merry for Mr Howieson's taste.

'What happened to your job in Aitchison's?' she asked.

Dick Aitchison was a local ironmonger.

'To tell you the truth, Betty, he's always pestering me to marry him.'

Aitchison, a widower, was no oil-painting, but he was jolly, like Katie herself, and his business was prosperous.

'Well, why not, Katie?'

'He's not my type.'

Both women laughed, but Mrs Blackwood wondered what Katie's type was. She hadn't known Jim Sellars, who had died about ten years ago when Katie was forty. So bonny and cheerful a woman must have had offers. Why had she turned them all down? Was it loyalty to her dead husband? Or was she, God help her, waiting for Prince Charming?

'I've always loved the smell of new shoes,' said Katie. 'This is such a lovely shop too.'

There was blue wall-to-wall carpeting. The chairs customers sat in were leather and chrome.

'A lot more elegant than selling paraffin and nails.'

Mrs Sellars was laughing at her own remark when Mr Howieson came through from the back-shop, frowning at such hilarity.

'This is Mrs Sellars,' said Mrs Blackwood. 'She's come to enquire about the job.'

'I see.' Still frowning, he studied the little widow. She tried hard to look demure.

Mrs Blackwood expected him to say curtly that Katie wasn't what he had in mind, but no, though he kept on frowning, he asked her to come with him into the back-shop.

As she went Katie waggled her fingers behind her back, it was her way of asking Mrs Blackwood to pray for her.

Mrs Blackwood hoped that Katie got the job for she would be cheerful company, but it was most unlikely. Mr Howieson had said that he wanted a tall, quiet, serious woman of good appearance. There was nothing wrong with Katie's appearance, except that her eyes were too lively and her cheeks too red, but she wasn't tall or quiet or serious.

None the less when she emerged at least ten minutes later – Mrs Blackwood sold a pair of shoes in the interim – she was beaming, which was very unusual in any woman who had been alone with Mr Howieson for that length of time. Mrs Traquair had sometimes come out of the back-shop pale-faced and trembling.

'Got it, Betty,' she whispered. 'Full-time, too. Start on Monday.'

'Well done, Katie.' But Mrs Blackwood couldn't help wondering how it had been done. Still, it was obvious that Katie needed the money. What she was wearing, a grey coat and red tammy, suited her, but the materials were cheap. As for her shoes it was astonishing that Mr Howieson had engaged someone wearing such bauchles.

*   *   *

Four weeks later two of Mrs Sellars' friends, Jean Kelly and Agnes McGhee, were having lunch with her in the Cosy Corner tearoom, as was their custom every Wednesday. They always looked forward to her amusing accounts of life in Holy Herbert's shoe shop. This afternoon she was wearing new shoes that looked as if they must have cost her half a week's wage. It wasn't like her to be so extravagant or indeed so vain.

'New shoes, Katie?' asked Jean.

'Very swish,' said Agnes.

'Herbert let me have them at cost price.'

'Herbert?' said Jean. 'So it's Herbert now?'

It wasn't easy to tell when Katie was blushing, because of the redness of her cheeks, but her friend saw that her neck was red too. 'I'm telling a lie,' she said, not looking at them. 'It wasn't cost price. They were a present, a birthday present. Last Friday was my birthday.'

'I clean forgot,' said Jean.

'So did I,' said Agnes.

'Many happy returns,' both said.

'My fiftieth,' said Katie.

'You could pass for forty,' said Jean, who was fifty-five and knew she looked it. 'What came over him? Did you let him feel your bum?' She could be very coarse at times.

'He would never do anything like that,' said Katie. Did she say it wistfully?

'He hasn't got the balls for it,' said Jean.

'Mary Traquair said she often thought he was dying to feel hers,' said Agnes.

'He's asked me out,' said Katie.

Her friends were astounded.

'To a prayer meeting?' asked Agnes, sarcastically.

'It's in the church hall. A professor's coming to give a lecture on missionary work in India.'

'My God!' Jean almost jabbed her chin with her fork.

'You're kidding, Katie,' said Agnes.

'No, I'm not. It could be very interesting. He's showing slides.'

'You'll never be able to keep your face straight,' said Jean.

'You never can,' said Agnes, 'when hypocrites are talking.'

Katie just smiled.

They stared at her, nonplussed. They had never seen her smile like that before. They had thought they knew her inside out, but here she was mystifying them.

'Do you think, Agnes,' said Jean, 'that that beautiful silvery hair has got to her?'

'Or could it be that three-bedroomed bungalow with the red roof?'

'I like him,' said Katie, with determination.

'How can you, Katie?' asked Jean. 'He's a bigot, a prude, and a creep.'

Agnes lowered her voice as a hint to Jean to lower hers. 'I'm told he made his wife's life a misery. The poor woman was glad to die to get away from him.'

'I've heard that too,' said Jean.

'His daughter's fond of him,' said Katie. 'She wouldn't be if he had been cruel to her mother.'

'From what I hear,' said Jean, 'his daughter's an insufferable puke.'

'His own son can't stand him,' said Agnes.

'He's got lots of good qualities,' said Katie, 'but they're all shut up in him.'

'And what's the cause of that?' asked Jean.

Katie hesitated. 'Religion, I think.'

'Isn't religion supposed to bring out all your good qualities?' asked Agnes.

'He takes it too seriously,' said Katie. 'He takes everything too seriously. That's his trouble. He could be made all right by somebody who understood him and liked him.'

'Are you telling us you think you're that somebody?' asked Jean.

'I'm not sure.'

Her friends stared at each other. 'I believe this lassie's serious,' said Jean. 'It sounds like it,' said Agnes.

'Some lassie,' said Katie.

'What age is he?' asked Agnes.

'Sixty-two, but he could pass for fifty-two.'

'*Are* you serious?' asked Jean.

Katie nodded. She seemed to her friends then child-like, too hopeful and too trusting.

'Well, I'm dumbfooner'd,' said Jean, 'as my grannie used to say.'

'Me too,' said Agnes.

Katie had turned pale. They could see that she was trembling.

'Is *he* serious?' asked Agnes, after a pause.

'I don't know.'

'Come off it, Katie,' said Jean. 'A woman can always tell if a man's serious about her. Has he made a pass at you?'

Katie was blushing again. Her friends stared at her, incredulously. Was she going to confess that she and Holy Herbert had been naughty on the blue carpet, among the shoe boxes?

'He helped me to try on the shoes,' she said.

Her friends laughed, in relief. That was more like their old Katie. They knew that men could show their interest in women in ridiculous ways.

'Don't tell anybody,' said Katie. 'I mean, there's nothing settled.'

'All right, hen,' said Jean. 'We'll keep it secret. But for God's sake don't enter into anything that could break your heart.'

'He's a good Christian,' said Katie.

That would have ended any conversation. They began to talk about a forthcoming dance at the golf club.

Herbert had no intimates to whom he could unburden his soul. There was only God. He wrote it down in a notebook which he kept in a locked drawer in his bedroom, safe from the prying eyes of his charwoman. He was letting the Lord know, although of course the Lord already knew. He strove to be humble and calm but could not help sometimes being arrogant and passionate. All the recent entries were about Mrs Sellars.

'Her mind is banal. Her conversation consists entirely of gossip. Her ignorance of Scriptures is dreadful, yet she feels no shame. She makes jests about it. She reads vulgar newspapers and foolish novels. She uses cheap scent. She giggles. Her bottom is fat. I should despise her, and I do. Why then is her presence in my shop a joy to me? Why do I pine in misery until I see her again? Why do I yearn to touch her, to stroke her soft white neck? It is no use reading Scriptures to blot her out of my mind. I see her face on the page. I hear her voice prattling nonsense. Three times have I had her dismissal notice ready. I know I am not the first godly man to be ensnared by an unworthy woman. Are there not instances in the Bible?'

'Tonight I stood in the rain for a whole hour outside the close where she lives, waiting to see if she came out. I intended to follow her to find out if she has an interest in some other man. Jealousy degrades. I feel degraded and yet I feel uplifted too. How is this possible? Before I left I kissed the filthy cold stone at the entrance to the close. In all my life I have never done a thing so incomprehensible and foolish. What is she after all? A small stupid woman with no dignity.'

'Mrs Sellars was here this evening. I do not know why I invited her or why she accepted the invitation. I showed her round the house. She was enthusiastic, but then so she is about so many things, whereas I myself am able to be enthusiastic about nothing. It is why I despise her and yet at the same time envy her and want to be with her. Even the Bible has lost its savour for me since she came into my life. She dared to say that my house was too dull and suggested ways of brightening it. She was wearing a blue costume. God help me, I kept wishing to see her naked. To such an extent have I been corrupted.'

'I have mentioned Mrs Sellars to my daughter Rachel who lives in Helensburgh. We keep in touch by telephone. She warned me against her, calling her a nobody and accusing her of being interested only in my house and shop. She would not, she said, come to the wedding, if it ever reached that length. She was quite hysterical about it.'

'I have had a letter from my son Edward. It seems Rachel has written to him about Mrs Sellars, seeking his help in turning me against her. But he urges me to go ahead, even if Mrs Sellars is as common as Rachel said. She might cure me. Cure me of what? He did not say, but of course I knew. He thinks I have some deficiency because I try to lead a Christian life. That is the kind of world we live in today, a son encourages his father to be a whoremonger. Purity is considered a disease.'

'This evening Katherine introduced me to her daughter Fiona. She is twenty years of age and a student at a Teachers' Training College in Dundee. She struck me as a sensible girl, ambitious to do well. Unlike so many teachers today she tries to speak properly and grammatically. She is at times impatient with her mother's chattering, as I am myself. She wishes, as I do, that her mother would be more serious. Yet if Katherine was serious would she attract me so much?'

'Today I asked Katherine to be my wife. She consented, too readily, as if she had been waiting for me to propose. Has she lured me into it, as Rachel suspects? Why should she, who laughs so much, wish to be joined to me who never laughs at all? I have warned her that Margaret, my previous wife, and I slept in separate rooms for years. She was not deterred. That would be taken care of, she said, meaning I do not know what. The wedding will be in St Cuthbert's. Mr Henderson has said he would be pleased to officiate. He thinks I did not treat Margaret well. He hinted that I could make amends by being very kind to Katherine. He does not understand. I have warned Katherine. She says she knows and it does not matter. What is it that she thinks she knows?'

Jean and Agnes had a long talk on the telephone about their newly betrothed friend.

'Isn't it awful, Agnes? What's the silly woman thinking about?

'Well, she warned us, didn't she?'

'I'm afraid for her, Agnes. I really am.'

'Afraid? What do you mean?'

'He's the kind you read about in the papers cutting their wives to pieces with an axe.'

'For heaven's sake, Jean!'

'It's repressed sex causes it. For years he's been desperate for it, yet he thinks it's filthy. When he gets it he blames the woman, in this case Katie.'

'My God, Jean, I hope you're wrong.'

'I hope myself I'm wrong. Why is she doing it, Agnes?'

'Well, she did tell us she likes him.'

'How could any woman like that cold-blooded hypocrite?'

'Maybe she thinks she can help him not to be cold-blooded or a hypocrite.'

'Katie's a nice little soul but she's never been what you'd call smart, has she?'

'She's not stupid, Jean.'

'No, but she's a bit simple. I've heard you say so yourself, Agnes.'

'Yes, I'd agree that she can be a bit simple at times. It's one of the nicest things about her.'

'So it is, but not this time. This time it's led her into this mess. She's had a hard time since Jim died, bringing up Fiona and giving Fiona everything she wanted, which has been quite a lot. So when she saw the chance of moving into a fine big house and having plenty of money for a change she couldn't resist it, without bothering about the price she might have to pay. Fiona's probably encouraged her. She's a young snob and would much rather live in a bungalow in Hillview Avenue than up a close in Wallace Street.'

'You could be right, Jean. Did we do all we could to stop her?'

'What more could we have done? Heaven knows we never praised Herbert.'

'We could have kept popping into the shop and showing him what vulgar friends she had.'

'He knew that. I wouldn't be surprised if he told her to have nothing to do with us. Has it been my imagination or has she been avoiding us a bit lately?'

'It's been your imagination, Jean. Katie would never avoid her friends. She's been busy. A woman about to be married has a lot to do. I suppose we'll be invited to the wedding. Will you go if we are?'

'I'm inclined to say no, Agnes. It would be like giving our blessing to something we think's all wrong.'

'That's one way of looking at it.'

'What other way is there?'

'Well, Jean, we would be letting her down, at a time when she needs all the support she can get. I think we should go.'

'We haven't been invited yet. Herbert might not want us.'

'Katie will insist. She can be very stubborn when she likes.'

'Bill says to count him out.' Bill was Jean's husband. 'He likes Katie but can't stand Herbert.'

'Archie's not very keen either, but he'll go to please me and for Katie's sake. It's on a Saturday morning. He says there's a golf competition on then. But he's fond of Katie.'

'Tell me any man that knows her who isn't fond of her. I'm sure she's had a dozen offers. So why choose Holy Herbert?'

'It could be love, Jean.'

'Don't make me laugh. My God, imagine being in bed with that pious creep. It's bad enough with a normal man, God knows.'

Agnes laughed. 'Well, anyway, we'll have to give her all the support we can.'

'I'm thinking of giving her as a wedding present a sachet stuffed with garlic. If you remember it kept Dracula at bay.'

'Jean, you're terrible. Right enough, it'll not be easy to think of a present. She'll have everything in that house.'

'Except affection. Be seeing you, Agnes. Must go. Master calls.'

'Be seeing you, Jean.'

The wedding took place less than four months after Mrs Sellars began working in the shoe shop. In the church there were some, including the groom's daughter, whose smiles of congratulation to the bride were mixed with suspicion and dislike. These ghouls, as Jean Kelly called them, evidently thought that poor Herbert had been ensnared by the sly little schemer. She and Agnes McGhee watched and listened with indignation. It astonished and angered them that anyone could think ill of Katie who was quite radiant that afternoon, in a pale blue costume, with her cheeks as red as the roses she was carrying. She seemed to be unaware of the animosity towards her. During the ceremony Jean felt an urge to shout out and object, but her husband Bill, out of the corner of his mouth, told her for Christ's sake to keep quiet, couldn't she see how happy Katie was? When the couple were pronounced man and wife and the groom kissed the bride, Jean whispered that it reminded her of a vulture pecking at a dead sheep. Beside her Agnes was on edge. She saw what Jean meant and there was certainly something rather horrible about that kiss, but it was very unfair to liken Katie to a dead sheep, for she looked not only bonnier than Agnes had ever seen her before but happier too. Maybe she knew what she was doing better than any of them. Simple people sometimes succeeded where clever ones failed. Nobody really knew Howieson. He was a very remote man. If Katie thought she could get close to him and bring out the good qualities which she thought were locked up in him then good luck to her.

Bride and groom slipped away from the reception in the Royal Hotel, leaving their guests to enjoy themselves. The most boisterous were the Kellies and the McGhees. They had not intended to be present but in the church they had been approached by Eddie Howieson and his wife, congenial souls, who had prevailed on them to come and keep them company. 'You're the only lot here that look human.' Their end of the long table had affronted the more temperate other end with their boozy hilarity.

In his glittering green Volvo, on their way to the five-star hotel in the Borders where they were to spend their honeymoon, Herbert rebuked his wife for having such rowdy and bibulous friends.

'I hope you will be seeing less of them from now on.'

Her reply was simple but resolute. 'No, Herbert. I shall see as much of them as I wish to.'

'Suppose I forbid it?'

She had known that it was going to be difficult. She had
worked out her strategy. It was based on her belief that
deep down Herbert wanted people to like him but was too
frightened to show it. What he was frightened of she did not
know but was determined to find out, she was sure it had to
do with religion. It seemed to her that religion ought to make
people happier, not more miserable; otherwise what was the
use of it?

'You'll like them when you get to know them,' she said.

She took hold of his arm because it was part of her plan to
touch him often, to help him get over his aversion to being
touched, even by her.

He shook off her hand. 'Not when I'm driving,' he muttered.

'I'm sorry.'

It was a twisty bit of road.

For the next few miles she debated with herself whether or
not to put her hand, light as a butterfly, on his thigh. After all,
in a few hours they would be in bed together. She had packed
two nightdresses, one white, opaque, and ankle-length, the
other black, transparent, and very short.

She decided against putting her hand on his thigh.

They passed a ruined abbey. Herbert told her its history.
Hundred of years ago monks had been butchered there. It
was interesting, but not really an appropriate subject for a
couple on honeymoon.

They crossed a bridge associated with Robert Burns. She
pointed that out and was given a lecture on what a reprobate
Burns had been.

'He was a fornicator.'

She couldn't deny it but the impish thought occurred to
her that she wouldn't have minded a little fornication with
the man who had written *Afton Water*. She hummed part of
the tune.

'He was a drunkard and a ne'er-do-well.'

She didn't know whether or not Burns had drunk too much but it struck her as ridiculous to call a man a ne'er-do-well whose statue was in cities all over the world.

Every honeymoon, she supposed, was bound to be something of an ordeal, but this one especially, with the groom contradicting the bride at every turn and grueing whenever she touched him.

She remembered her last honeymoon, twenty-four years ago. It had been spent in a small boarding-house in Edinburgh. They hadn't travelled in a swanky car but in a crowded train. She had been nervous then too, but for very different reasons.

He saw the tears in her eyes. 'It has always been a mystery to me why women weep at weddings. Are they not supposed to be happy occasions?'

'Sometimes when you're happy the only way you can show it is by crying.'

'That sounds very like nonsense.'

'What do *you* think marriage is, Herbert?'

'It is a holy sacrament, made in the sight of God.'

She was sorry she had asked.

'It is a time for making vows, of fidelity, of meekness before God, and chastity.'

Oh God, she thought. Chastity? 'Yes, Herbert.'

'There were once Christian sects where after marriage the wedded couple were not permitted to see each other for a month.'

'What was the purpose of that, Herbert?'

'Need you ask? It was so that by abstinence they showed their awareness that marriage was essentially a spiritual relationship.'

Abstinence sounded hopeful. You had to abstain from something. What did he think that something was?

'Otherwise it is nothing but a licence for lust.'

'Yes, Herbert.'

'A man ought not to marry a woman because he lusts after her body or a woman because she lusts after a man's.'

'No, Herbert.'

Still, it wasn't as if he was a monk. He had been married before. She had something to work on.

The hotel had once been a nobleman's country house. There were extensive grounds with woods and gardens. As they drove up the long driveway they saw deer among the trees, and near the large impressive building a peacock with its tail outspread. A servant, almost as resplendent, in a red jacket and blue trousers, came down the steps to carry in their cases. He would also garage the car. This was five-star treatment. Katie was determined not to be intimidated. Compared to the test that would confront her in an hour or two's time this present trial, of meeting well-off people and supercilious servants, was easy. In the big hall were marble statues. One was of a naked woman with one arm covering her bosom and the other what Jean Kelly would have called her dainty. Another was of a man, naked too, but with a fig leaf.

They hadn't just a bedroom but a sitting-room too, and a bathroom of their own. Buckingham Palace, she thought, couldn't be grander. Surely Herbert wouldn't have spent so much money if he really believed that marriage should be purely spiritual. Wasn't spending lots of money rather vulgar? She decided she'd wear the black nightie.

They had dinner by candlelight in a quiet corner of the dining-room. On the wall above them was a large painting of naked nymphs in a wood. Katie could see it but Herbert's back was to it. Perhaps we should change places, she thought.

He was for waving away the wine waiter but she put out her hand for the list. She knew nothing about wine, but if it was dear it was likely to be good. They were all dear, with none under £10. She chose one at £10.50.

'You will come to expensive places, darling,' she whispered. 'Anyway, this is a very special occasion. Isn't it?'

He gave a wincing sort of smile and a shaky sort of nod.

The meal was the best she had ever had in her whole life, and was served with elegance. Whatever happened afterwards she was enjoying herself now, and so she ate and drank with relish, prattled happily, and felt more and more loving and amorous. Looking round the dining-room at other men in it she saw with pride that none was as aristocratic-looking as her Herbert. He could have been taken for the nobleman who had once owned this splendid house.

She was pleased, for his sake, that some of the men had given her and were still giving her admiring, not to say desirous, glances. She was sure that she did look desirable, especially now that she was flushed with wine, affection, and anticipation. She could not have said, however, truthfully, that Herbert looked eager to go dashing upstairs to bed. Indeed, she could imagine Jean Kelly saying that he looked as if he was going to be hanged. For heaven's sake, Katie, she warned herself, this is no time for a sense of humour.

He said little and she had no idea what he was thinking or feeling. Once, as she glanced up at the carefree nymphs, she felt a pang of terror. What if she was wrong and there were no good qualities locked up in him waiting to be released? What if the Herbert that Jean and Agnes, and others, knew, was the real, the only Herbert? What if the stories about his callousness to his first wife were true? What evidence did she have for thinking that there was another Herbert, who might not make the best husband in the world but who could be made as good as any? Only a sadness in his eyes that had always vanished as soon as he saw that she had noticed it. Sadness that had in it an appeal. He wanted her help and needed her. It was not much to gamble all her future happiness on, but she did not regret it, she was still sure that she had made the right decision.

After dinner, since it was still daylight, he suggested, with desperation in his voice, a stroll in the grounds. It was as if he was putting off his hanging.

It would be like a hanging if she lost confidence. With her own voice as steady as she could manage she replied that it had been a long tiring day for both of them and if he didn't mind she'd rather that they went straight to bed.

'You'd better use the bathroom first, darling,' she said. 'I'll take longer than you.'

'Very well.' He disappeared into the bathroom, carrying his pyjamas, neatly folded. His fetish for tidiness, which irritated Betty Blackwood in the shop, didn't bother Katie, although she herself was inclined to leave things lying about to be tidied up later. If Herbert wanted her to be tidier, well, she would be.

Soon he returned. He had brushed his hair, in the style that she had said she liked, not flat but wavy. It was a good sign. His pyjamas were old-fashioned, white with thin red stripes. She could not tell, for he did not smile or speak, whether he had taken out his dental plate. Like her he had three false teeth, at the front. She had been wondering about her own. Should she leave them in and avoid unromantic gaps?

'Won't be long, darling,' she said.

He didn't look as if he would mind if she took an hour or even two. He had produced a small black book, a Bible she felt sure, and had begun to read it. That was all right. Perhaps it was his way of preparing for love.

In the bathroom she undressed and then studied her body in the full-length mirror. The smallness of her breasts, which once had disappointed her, was now pleasing. Big ones saggd

67

and might have put Herbert off. Her belly bulged a little; a delicious roundness, anyone who loved her would say. Her bottom was plump and saucy. But her legs and feet were her most attractive assets. What a pity they played no visible part in love-making.

Her hair, arranged in what she called her Nefertiti fringe, was still dark and lustrous. She counted half a dozen white ones, and then quickly gave up, because really there were hundreds. At the side of her nose was a tiny blackhead that she must have missed last night. She didn't have time to squeeze it out; in any case it would have made her hose red. That left her teeth. She hated going to bed with her dental plate in her mouth for she was afraid of swallowing it in her sleep and choking to death, but it would be better to take that chance rather than run the risk of discouraging Herbert with gap-toothed smiles.

Should she dash out naked and jump into bed before he had time to protest? No, better put on the black nightie, which after all hid nothing.

Good luck, she whispered to herself in the mirror. She felt like a ballet dancer about to prance out on to the stage.

Not on tiptoe exactly, but taking quick little steps, she ran out and twirled in front of him.

'How do you like your new wife, Herbert?' she simpered.

She felt silly but saw from his face that she was on the right lines.

It was proper for him to see her nakedness; the book in his hand had given him that permission. He would have been proud of her daintiness, if pride had not been sinful. He could not be sorry for himself, that would have been unmanly.

All that she read in his face.

As he strove to find the right Christian reaction she skipped across and was in bed beside him before he could beg or order her not to. Gently she took the book from his hand – yes, it was a Bible – and dropped it on the carpet. Then she lay on her side staring wistfully and lovingly up at him.

Slowly he slipped down until he was lying beside her, gazing at her face inches from his own. He would see the white hairs and the blackhead, but it couldn't be helped. He would also see love and wonder in her eyes. In his what did she see? Fear? Anxiety? Disgust? Yes, but also sadness and appeal. He was saying nothing, except for an occasional gasp, but he was really crying to her for help, pity, and love.

'Herbert darling,' she murmured. Under the bedclothes her hand was tender, purposeful, and brave. 'What is it the Bible says? Made one flesh?'

He muttered something. It sounded like 'Filthy temptress' but surely couldn't have been. Then he groaned it again.

She could have taken it seriously and their marriage would have ruined from the start, but her sense of humour came to her rescue. Pretend, it said, that he meant it humorously; pretend that he was making a joke.

'That's right,' he whispered. 'Like Eve.'

And, like Adam, he succumbed.

She helped him, unofficiously. He had to be made to feel that in this part of the sacrament he was master, as no doubt somewhere in the Bible it said he should be. For the same reason the pleasure must be all his. There would be other times.

It was going to be all right, she thought. Here she was making a loving husband of him. In time she would make a human being of him. She might even teach him how to laugh.

She took care not to laugh herself when, the consummation over, he asked, humbly, if she would mind praying with him to thank the Lord. She still didn't laugh when she realised he meant on their knees, on the floor, side by side. She just did what he asked and didn't grumble when the praying went on too long and her knees began to ache, in spite of the thick carpet. After all, she herself had something to thank the Lord for.

Doreen and the Virgin Plumber

D OREEN'S LADIES' HAIRDRESSING SALON in Gourock Avenue, just off the main street, was the best appointed, the most up-to-date, and the most expensive in town. Men, catered for on Thursday evenings, jested that it reminded them of a high-class French brothel, with its perfumes, its gaudy colours, its glitter, and above all its proprietrix, with her enamelled face, gorgeous smocks, and Madame de Pompadour wigs. Since she had not been born in the town but had come from Glasgow when she was in her twenties years and years ago her age was not exactly known and was not easily guessed. Her face was a masterpiece of artifice, making it ageless, and her body was slim enough to have been a girl of sixteen's. Moreover she had two voices, one harsh and dominant, showing her to be a match for the tough world, and the other soft and winsome, as if she was a wee lost girl wanting everybody to be kind to her.

That she had lovers was not in doubt; how many, however, was. Men who bragged that they had done great feats in her bed were never near it. Even before the break-up of her marriage, while she and Tony were supposed to be living amicably together, she had had affairs, though never more than one at a time. Tony had slept around, but it hadn't been that which had caused her to throw him out; she admitted the mote in her own eye. It had been his drinking, and not that by itself either, for she liked a drink herself. It had been his thriftlessness. His father had left him a prosperous builder's business. Wishing to be an artist – he had spent two years at Glasgow School of Art – Tony had quickly sold it and at once set about squandering the proceeds. It was then that he met and married Doreen who had come to Lunderston to work as a hairdresser. She had made sure that she got her hands on enough of the money to buy her business in Gourock Avenue, and also that they held on to the villa in the East Bay that had belonged to his parents. Tony himself had bought a good-going pub, the Red Deer, but within a few years was bankrupt, largely through drinking with and treating customers. When he had begun to sponge off her she had had enough. Twice she had cast him off and twice he had come cringing back. Now he was gone, for good this time, she vowed. If asked where he was she would reply, in her toughest voice, 'Timbuktu, for all I care.' But he was really in Glasgow, managing a pub for a fat woman of sixty, and among his duties was sleeping with her.

Doreen was convinced that the reason for her youthful appearance and her sharpness of mind was sexual satisfaction, though she would have given it a more romantic name, and she had learned, through experience, that in spite of what so-called experts on sexual matters wrote in women's magazines, size did matter, especially if accompanied by youthful zest and vigour.

With her in the villa by the Firth lived her fifteen-year-old daughter Melanie, and her mother who was seventy-seven and senile. The latter was too benighted to notice, let alone object, and the former too broadminded, when Doreen entertained a boy-friend, which usually meant her going to bed with him.

She still hoped to find a man so desirable that she would want to marry him, Tony having been flushed away. He would have to be at least ten years younger than herself, handsome, but not effeminately so, generous, but not indiscriminately, amorous, but only towards her, convivial, but no beer-belly, comfortably off, but not necessarily owning a Rolls Royce, and above all virile, for she would be relying on him to keep her young, in appearance and spirit, more than she would on wigs, cosmetics, and slimming aids. Indeed, when she was between lovers and hadn't had sex for a month or so she began to feel panicky, like someone with a wonky heart who had lost his pills.

She was in that nervous and anxious condition when she met young Simon McKay. It was two days before Christmas. There had been a spell of Arctic weather. The pipes in the shop were frozen, at her busiest time of the year. Plumbers had more work than they could cope with. When she telephoned Mr McKay he said he would send his son Simon who, though only nineteen, was competent to do the job. 'I don't care if you send King Kong,' she said, 'so long as he can unfreeze my pipes.'

But when Simon came, with his bag of tools, though he was tall and powerfully built, he was no simian monster. Doreen could see that he was no Einstein either, and wasn't surprised when he confessed, with a candid smile, that he had once sawn through the wrong pipes and almost electrocuted himself, but with his fair hair, smooth skin, powerful thighs, and ingenuous gaze he was, she thought, with her heart beating faster, fitted to unthaw pipes more intimate than those under the floor of her shop. Those strong haunches might not be convenient for crawling into holes as plumbers often had to do, but they were very suitable for another purpose that she had immediately in mind. He would be the youngest she had ever had, and the most innocent. She felt certain that he was still a virgin, for, as he worked, he chatted about having been a scout and having won prizes in the Bible Class.

When he was leaving she whispered to him that there was a tap in her bathroom that needed a new washer. Could he come and fix it, that evening, at eight o'clock, say? Did he know where she lived? She would be very grateful.

Simon was not all that simple, though his sisters in childhood had called him so, from the nursery rhyme. He thought he knew what Doreen really wanted of him and he was more than eager to oblige her, provided that no one ever found out. In spite of his bigness and strength he was timid when it came to behaviour that his mother, or Mr Henderson the minister, or Mr Sinclair his old scoutmaster, would call immoral. Once, egged on by friends, on the beach behind some parked boats, he had put his hand up Lizzie McLean's clothes, while she had her hand inside his trousers. 'Leaky big eedjit,' she had said, philosophically. 'Some plumber you'll make.' And she had borrowed his handkerchief. He remembered that episode with shudders of shame mixed with thrills of delight, but he had attempted no girl since, not because he was keeping himself pure for the girl he would marry one day, as Mr Henderson exhorted, but because he lacked confidence. He had been waiting for the kind of opportunity that had now come; a woman as old as his mother, not a giggly impatient girl, who would show him how to do it, just as his mother had shown him in his infancy how to use his potty. It would be done in comfort too, not on hard pebbles with gulls screeching.

So at twenty to eight, wearing his sheepskin coat, with an assortment of washers and a shifting spanner in the pocket just in case, and a woollen Balaclava such as IRA men wore, he left the house, after telling his mother that he was going along to Bruce Street to help his friend James Monro to assemble a model of a Harrier Jump Jet. She was satisfied, for James's mother was a past president of Lunderston Ladies' Business

Club. Neither lady was to know that though their sons did, in James's room, work on models they also studied magazines full of coloured pictures of naked young women. James was able to collect such magazines for he had no sisters to pry into his secrets and his mother was too busy with her various duties. To be truthful, Simon was never easy in his mind when poring over those big breasts and hairy pudenda. He couldn't help feeling that he was somehow betraying his mother and dishonouring his sisters. Did not Mr Henderson call the human body the vessel of the Holy Spirit, to be regarded with reverence and kept pure? He had been shocked when James had taken out his Peter (which was what Simon's mother had called it when he was a toddler) and pressed it against one of the women who had her legs wide open. He had challenged Simon to do likewise, but Simon had shyly refused, though he could not help thinking, with guilty pride, that his Peter, in the same state, was a good deal bigger than James's.

There was an icy wind blowing off the Firth. Streets were slippery and deserted. As he walked along the sea-front it was as if he was alone in the world, except for Doreen waiting for him. Approaching her villa, called The Roses, he stopped under a lamp to look at his wrist-watch. Though he knew the jokes about plumbers always being late he did not want to be too early for this appointment, which after all might not involve plumbing. When he reached the gate he walked past. It was only five to eight. Snow was beginning to fall. The moisture from his mouth on the Balaclava felt as if it was turning to ice. His shivers, though, were not all caused by cold.

What if Doreen had been joking and wasn't expecting him? What if it was her daughter Melanie who opened the door? He would feel a terrible fool standing on the doorstep, mumbling that he had come to fix the tap in the bathroom. Mr Henderson had once said in a sermon that a man ought not to be afraid to look a fool, but he had meant when doing God's work.

Exactly at eight he rang the door bell. Faintly, because of the wind, he heard the St Cuthbert church clock striking in the distance. He thought of the big Christmas tree outside it, all lit up.

To his relief it was Doreen herself who came to the door, wearing a long pink housecoat and pink furry slippers. She seemed to be expecting him, and yet she looked surprised too.

'Come about the washer,' he muttered.

'Of course, Simon. Come in. You look frozen. Is it snowing?' She knocked some flakes off his shoulder.

In the hall, lit by a red bulb, she helped him off with his coat. 'What a weight!' she said.

'There's a shifting-spanner in the pocket.'

'A what?' She laughed. 'Taking no chances, were you?'

Under the coat he had on his best green cords and his green Pringle pullover. He had put on clean underwear and fresh socks.

She led him into a large sitting-room, which was warm and cosy. Would they do it here? he wondered. There was a sheepskin rug in front of the gas fire, and the sofa, on which he sat, was long enough but perhaps not broad enough.

'What about a wee drinkie to warm you up?' she asked.

He had already smelled whisky off her breath.

'Yes, thanks.'

'Whisky?'

He hated whisky. 'Whisky would do fine, thanks.'

'With water?'

'Sure, with water.'

He noticed that she gave him more water than whisky and herself more whisky than water. Was it because he was only nineteen? Or could there be some other reason?

He had heard that if a man was too drunk he couldn't make love.

Under the housecoat Doreen seemed to have very little on. Certainly her legs were bare. They were very nice legs for a woman as old as she. How old was that? He had once heard his mother say scornfully, 'That Doreen must be at least forty-five.' He blushed as he caught a glimpse of her breasts. They seemed genuine, though there were rumours that she wore falsies. She'd loosened some of the buttons of her housecoat.

She sat beside him on the sofa. 'Tell me more about yourself, Simon,' she said, using her soft, winsome voice. 'I know you were a Scout and won prizes in the Bible Class, but what about girls? I bet you've broken lots of hearts.'

'Not really.'

'With those lovely curls?'

'I play badminton a lot.'

She laughed. 'You must look a smasher in those short white short. I mean, with legs like yours.'

'I play rugby too.'

'Should you, Simon? You could break that beautiful nose.' She touched it with a finger-tip. 'Isn't it a rough game? They stamp on players on the ground, and they're not particular what parts they stamp on either. Isn't that so?'

He nodded. 'Only dirty players do that.'

She put her arm round his neck. Her perfume had his head swimming. 'Tell me, Simon, did you really come to fix my tap?'

He grinned and made a gesture with his head, half a nod and half a shake.

'So you had something else in mind? May I ask what?'

He blushed. 'I don't like to say.'

'Is it something best done in bed?'

He nodded.

'I think I know what it is, Simon. Well, shall we go upstairs?'

'Yes, please.' He could hardly speak, his mouth was so dry. The whisky hadn't helped.

The staircase had thick carpet on it, so he didn't have to tiptoe, but he did, for he had the same feeling that he had in church. He wasn't drunk either, so he didn't have to hold on to the mahogany banister, but he did, for his legs were shaky. In front of him Doreen's bottom swayed from side to side.

Music was coming from above. It must be Melanie in an attic. She must like it up there, for it was a big house, with at least five bedrooms.

Doreen was gasping, and yet she had come up the stairs slowly. It must be because she smoked too much. She closed the door of her bedroom behind them.

He was so intent on looking at the big bed, pink like the rest of the room, that he wasn't aware she had removed her housecoat and whatever she had on beneath it, until she grabbed his hand and pulled him towards her. She was bare naked now. Her breasts weren't false, though they looked rather rubbery. She had a mole on her belly. His thoughts were disjointed because she was kissing him and at the same time unzipping his flies. He was in a curious state of mind, wanting her to feel how manly he was and yet wishing that she would not be so forward.

'My God, Simon!' she said, giving him a complimentary squeeze. 'Off with everything, lover boy.'

He did not mind the top garments, pullover, shirt, and singlet coming off, for he was proud of his torso and did exercises to keep it in good shape, but he was shy about what would be revealed when off came cords and underpants. He had often admired it in his own bedroom, but there had been no woman present.

Doreen and the Virgin Plumber

'My God, Simon, what a lovely Christmas present! Thank you very much.'

Seconds later they were in bed. It was warm, because the electric blanket had been switched on earlier. Doreen therefore had been hoping he would come. Her face now being so close to his he could not help noticing how thick the powder on it was, to hide wrinkles. Maybe she did not look forty-five but she certainly looked forty. Instead of being put off he felt reassured. This was not just fornication, a word Mr Henderson was fond of, it was also learning.

'Are you really a virgin?' she asked.

Should he boast of it or lie about it? He knew what his mother and Mr Henderson would have said but he was taken aback to find that Doreen agreed with them. 'That's marvellous, Simon. Imagine in this day and age still being a virgin at nineteen. And you so well-equipped too.'

He knew that he should be doing something, like fondling her breasts, so he did it.

'No need for that, lover,' she gasped. 'I'm as ready as I'll ever be. So up you get, cowboy.'

She helped to heave him up on top of her. Immediately all shyness left him. He felt not like a cowboy but a cavalry officer. Before, however, he could swing his sabre, as it were, he heard noises outside, mutterings, tappings, and shufflings. He grew stiff all over. Had his mother and Mr Henderson arrived, with the police?

'It's all right,' said Doreen, impatiently. 'It's just my mother getting up to go to the bathroom. She refuses to use a chamber pot. She's nearly eighty.'

'Will she be all right?'

'Of course she'll be all right.'

'She seems to be talking to somebody.'

'She talks to people who are dead. She lives in the past.

Your concern does you credit, Simon, but haven't you urgent business to attend to?'

'My grannie fell down the stairs in the dark. She broke her femur.'

'Well, it's not dark out there.'

'Does she know I'm here?'

'I told you, she's only interested in what happened years ago.'

'Your daughter Melanie, does she know I'm here?'

'I haven't sent the town crier round.'

'I told my mother I'd be home by ten.'

'Then we'll have to get a move on, won't we? That's it. Done the right way this is the most beautiful thing in the world, and, Simon, for a beginner you're doing it very well. Jesus, Simon, I'm in heaven.'

Vaguely he was displeased by her using Jesus's name at such a time, but he was very pleased that he had so soon got the hang of it. He remembered the first time he had driven a dodgem car at the Fair. He had been only seven or eight. He knew it was daft to think of that now but he couldn't help it. Then he was a spaceman, guiding his machine among the stars.

Even so Doreen must have been further off still, for she didn't hear what caused him to stop suddenly and lift his head.

'What's the matter?' she gasped. 'You can't take cramp at your age.'

'Somebody's come into the house.' Could it be his mother and Mr Henderson?

'Don't be silly. The door's locked. Nobody has a key. Nobody.' But her voice faltered.

They both listened. Somebody was creeping up the stairs, with many stumbles. Whoever it was seemed to be weeping.

'The bastard!' cried Doreen. 'No, it can't be. He wouldn't have the bloody nerve.'

'Who do you think it is?'

'My husband. He's the only one with a key. He shouldn't have. He was supposed to hand it over. The lying bastard said he'd lost it.'

'Will he be angry at seeing me here?'

'I'm the one that's angry. He's got no rights in this house, even if he was born in it. He got well paid for his share.'

'Should I hide somewhere?'

'You stay where you are, exactly where you are. I'll soon get rid of him.'

There was a tap on the door, an apologetic cough, a tearful snigger, and in crept a man of about fifty-five, his lank grey hair wet with melted snow. Held tightly by Doreen, Simon had to twist his neck to glance behind. He saw that Mr Saunders must have taken off his overcoat downstairs, for he was wearing a Harris tweed jacket with leather patches at the elbows, and fawn trousers soaked from the knees down. He sat on the chair where Simon had put his clothes and took off his shoes. His socks were sodden. He had a thin grey bony face. Simon remembered him. Mr Saunders had once drawn cartoons for the *Gazette*. It was said he could have been a successful artist but for his boozing.

He didn't seem to notice Simon or perhaps he was too polite to mention it.

'Come to spend Christmas with you and Melanie, pet,' he said.

'Like hell you are.'

'Christmas is a time for families to get together.'

So it was, thought Simon.

'How the hell did you get here?' asked Doreen. 'Did she throw you out?'

'It's a long story, pet, a long sad story.' At last he became aware of Simon. 'Good evening, friend,' he said.

'Good evening,' said Simon.

'Who are you, may I ask?'

'No, you may not,' said Doreen. 'He's here because I invited him, which is more than I can say about you.'

'That's no way to talk about the father of your child. Where is my little girl Melanie?'

'Don't you dare disturb her, you drunken bum. She doesn't want ever to see you again. Get that into your head. If it's money you want my purse is in the dressing-table drawer. Take ten pounds, all right make it twenty, and then go.'

'It's snowing, and I've got no where to go to.'

'One of your old girl friends will take you in.'

'They're all married, pet. Who's this then?'

'It's none of your business who he is.'

'I find a man in bed with my wife and I'm told it's none of my business?'

Simon wanted to apologise to them both and then take his leave. Unfortunately Doreen still held him and Mr Saunders was sitting on his clothes.

'In France,' said Tony,' if I was to shoot you both in the act I'd get off. Crime of passion, it would be called.' He felt through his pockets and then jumped up or tried to, for his legs were weak. 'Back in a minute.' Then he crept out of the room.

'Is he going for a gun?' asked Simon, alarmed.

'He hasn't got a gun.'

'I saw one hanging on the wall.'

'Oh, that. It's ornamental. Anyway it isn't loaded.'

'Are you sure?'

'Of course I'm sure. Even if it was loaded he wouldn't have the guts to shoot us. If I had a gun I'd shoot him, the sneaky bastard.'

'What's he gone out for then?'

'His fags. He doesn't only drink himself to death, he smokes himself to death too. I should have divorced the bastard years ago. Listen to him coughing. But why are we letting him spoil our pleasure. Resume, Simon, resume.'

'But what if he comes back?'

'Ignore him. Pretend he isn't there. My God, it's incredible you're still able. What it is to be young.'

Inspired by the compliment, Simon did his best. She squirmed and moaned, and dug her nails into his back. The pain somehow added to his pleasure. He felt triumphant.

Meanwhile Tony had come in and was sitting on the chair again, lighting a cigarette. He had to try his lighter about a dozen times before it worked. Coughing shook his whole body. What was going on in the bed did not seem to interest him.

Given permission and a push, Simon dismounted. For the first time he was facing Tony.

'You've got a fine big one there, Doreen,' said Tony. 'But you could be his mother. What age are you, sonny?'

'Don't answer him,' said Doreen. 'It's none of his business.'

But Simon was eager to tell someone that though only nineteen and hitherto a virgin he had just given proof of his virility. Tony seemed as sympathetic as anyone.

'I'm nineteen,' he said.

'Hardly out of the cradle. What do you do? Are you a student?'

'I'm a plumber. I work for my dad, Stevie Mckay.'

'Don't tell him anything,' said Doreen.

'A plumber? Mckay? Sure I remember you, or anyway your dad. I'm a Lunderston man, you know. Born and bred. This was my parents' house. I was born in it.

Simon glanced at his watch. It was twenty minutes to ten. He still had time to get home by ten and prevent his mother from pestering him with questions. He would have to tell her lies and he didn't like doing that; besides, he wasn't very good at it.

'The boy wants to go home,' said Tony. 'His mother will be getting anxious.'

'Mind your own fucking business,' said Doreen.

Simon was shocked. He hated to hear a woman using such language. He crawled out of bed, hiding his Peter with his hand.

'Excuse me, sir,' he said. 'You're sitting on my clothes.'

'Sorry.' Tony rose.

'Thank you.'

'Don't mention it.'

He was a polite well-mannered man who had been ruined by drink. Mr Henderson was always lecturing the Bible Class about the evils of alcohol. He could have used Mr Saunders as an example.

At last Simon was ready. He had put on his socks inside out and his underpants back to front but it didn't matter. He wasn't sure whether he should shake hands with Mr Saunders or give Doreen a farewell kiss. He just said 'I'll be going now,' and left. Outside the door he paused and heard Mr Saunders whining 'What about it pet? Can I come in beside you? Look, I'm shivering. I'm taking pneumonia. Heat me up as you used to. We'll just lie and talk. It's all I'm fit for, God knows. We'll talk about Christmases in the past when we were happy together and Melanie was wee.'

'Go to hell,' said Doreen, but not so contemptuously.

Just then another door opened and out came Doreen's old mother, in a white nightgown and blue cardigan. She was feeling her way with a walking-stick.

'Merry Christmas,' said Simon.

She didn't hear or see him. Muttering to the dead, she disappeared into the bathroom.

Doreen and the Virgin Plumber

Was there really, he wondered, a tap needing a new washer? As he ran downstairs and put on his coat and Balaclava and went out into the snow and freezing wind Simon's heart was ringing like bells. He felt goodwill towards everybody. This was going to be his merriest Christmas ever. He had been given a present that far transcended last Christmas's from his parents, a big transistor radio that could get China. He had been made a man. He wouldn't tell his friends about it, not just because his mother might get to know, but also because it was the kind of treasure you could keep to yourself without feeling selfish.

The Locked Lavatories

THE *Lunderston Gazette* IS published every Friday.
People queue up outside newsagents at noon to buy it.
No Bible is ever perused more devotedly. Every advertisement
– there are hundreds – is noted, every name in the Sheriff Court
report, and every item of local news. There is a correspondence
section called the Safety Valve. The editor, John Scobie, who is
also the proprietor, is able to allow more latitude than editors
of national newspapers, since the people of Lunderston are
united in calling a fool a fool, an incompetent an incompetent,
and a rogue a rogue, in public as well as in private. No one
has ever been sued, for both the defamed and the defamer
have their eyes on the truth and not on possible damages.
If someone sees or is made to see that he or she has made
a mistake or gone too far an apology is given and accepted,
which is the end of the matter. Similar misstatements in the
national press would have to be paid for with thousands of
pounds for the person in a huff and thousands more for the
lawyers in the case. Lunderston prefers to keep its quarrels to
itself. Sometimes, however, it is an outsider who starts the
pens writing.

Recently the following letter appeared.

'Dear Sir,

I and my friends have been coming on bus tours to your beautiful town for years. We have always been treated with courtesy and consideration. It is with sorrow therefore that I recount what happened to us during our most recent visit. As you know, Ardpatrick Point is a beauty spot about two miles out of Lunderston. There are seats on which to rest while enjoying the wonderful views of the mountains of Arran. I and my friends have often praised the council whose doing this is. This summer however we suffered a shock. The driver of our bus always takes us out to Ardpatrick Point where we enjoy the fine views and the sea breezes. Without being indelicate I would like to remind the good people of Lunderston that we are all pensioners. Some of us will never see eighty again. It is necessary for us to have a convenience handy. At Ardpatrick Point there is one, for Ladies and Gents, kept spotlessly clean by the gentleman who lives in a cottage nearby. Picture our amazement, and imagine our discomfort, when this summer we found both doors padlocked. We could not understand. A terrible mistake had been made. While we were wondering what to do and our driver was offering to drive us back into town, the gentleman aforesaid, the custodian, a pensioner himself, came out of his house and apologised to us. The doors were locked by order of the council. It was to save paying him the sum of £35 weekly to keep the toilets clean and in working order. We are loyal British subjects and wish to do what is best for our country, but surely this is a ridiculous economy. Mr Robertson kindly offered the ladies among us the use of his own toilet. The gentlemen had to scramble behind rocks on the shore. One, I may say, fell and injured his leg. What a disgrace! When we went back into town we found that of the three conveniences known to us only one, that near the pier, is open. What is the matter with Lunderston? Judging by the fine houses and gardens it is not a destitute town. We have always found it very hospitable. Now we find doors locked in our faces. I and my friends hope that by our next visit those padlocks will have been removed.

Yours sincerely,
Annie Murphy (Mrs)
President, Brownhill Old Peoples' Club
Manchester.'

The following week there were four letters on the subject.

'Dear Sir,

As the councillors representing Lunderston on the District Council, we would like to comment on Mrs Annie Murphy's letter anent the padlocking of the public lavatories, at Ardpatrick Point and elsewhere. We feel we owe it to ourselves to explain that at the meeting of the Council when this diabolical measure was passed – by only one vote! – we both not only voted against it but also spoke strongly against it. We pointed out that Lunderston as a holiday resort depended on visitors, and many of these, like Mrs Murphy and her friends, are elderly, a circumstance giving rise to certain frailties. We shall in the meantime name no names, but if we are not able to have this absurd decision overruled very soon we shall have no hesitation in letting the people of Lunderston know the councillors responsible for it. Our loyalties are to those who elected us.

Yours,
Councillor John Meek
Councillor Jack Rankin.'

'Dear Sir,

I take off my hat, or should I say my bonnet, to Mrs Annie Murphy. She is the kind of lady our country needs. She has seen an injustice and has not hesitated to expose it. May I describe how this locking of the lavatories has affected me? I am, as many of your readers will know, an old man. My age in fact is eighty-two. I am fortunate in that I still have the use of all my faculties, though a little deaf. My weakness is that I can last only so long before having to relieve myself. From my house to the newsagent's is for me a twelve minutes' walk. A younger man could do it in five. For years now every morning I have walked to the shop to fetch my newspaper. I have made grateful use of the toilet on Kirk Brae, close-by. Then I have enjoyed my walk back home. Some days ago I found the door padlocked. I could not believe it. I still find it difficult to believe. I no longer go for my newspaper myself. I dare not. My pattern of life has been upset. I am sure that there are others similarly affected. I put my case to the fair-minded people of Lunderston.

Yours faithfully,
Alec Sproat
10 Beech Crescent.'

'Dear Sir,

In reference to Mrs Annie Murphy's letter regarding the Council's recent furtive decision to close public lavatories in the interests of economy, my wife and I spent several weeks during last winter in the Algarve, Portugal. There we were pleasantly surprised, and if I may say so, relieved, to find the various towns well supplied with public lavatories for both "Homens" and "Senoras", all of them kept in immaculate condition. Yet Portugal is said to be the poorest country in Western Europe. Are not our political masters in London always assuring us that we are enjoying a higher standard of living than ever before? Yet we cannot afford to keep our public toilets open. The sooner we Scots are in control of our own affairs the better.

Yours,
Malcolm McPherson
24 Clyde Street.'

'Dear Sir,

As a ratepayer of Lunderston I write in connection with the letter written by Mrs Annie Murphy of Manchester. In the first place I think she should mind her own business. But I have to thank her for informing me that Mr Robertson received £35 per week for looking after two small lavatories. That is nearly £2000 per year, in my view an exorbitant sum. Therefore I applaud the Council for their decision to close the lavatories and so save ratepayers' money. I would like to suggest that all public lavatories be privatised. It is ridiculous in this day and age that they should be free. They are not free in Glasgow Central Station. Let them be put out to tender. The people buying them could charge a modest fee. I suggest 10p. With the profits they could be kept in good order and the Council would be saved an intolerable expense. Most people would agree that the lavatories in the past were dreary, smelly places. In private hands they could be made attractive. I speak as one who has never received a penny in charity from the Council or anyone else.

Yours indignantly,
Jennifer Kerr (Miss)
"Seaview", East Bay.'

Letters then poured in. The editor had to make a selection.

'Dear Sir,

As Convenor of the Committee of the District Council which voted, with great reluctance, to close certain public lavatories, not only in Lunderston be it understood, I feel it is my duty to give your readers the reason; in one word, shortage of funds. Leaving politics aside, it is a fact that Central Government cuts down allowances, while the public complains about rates increases. It seemed to some of us that since people nowadays use tearooms and coffee-shops so much, not to mention hotel bars, where there are toilet facilities, it would be a saving without too great inconvenience to close some of the lesser-used lavatories. Miss Kerr's suggestion that the lavatories be privatised was discussed at some length, but it was concluded that the difficulties would be too great. I should point out that this closing of these lavatories is intended as an experiment. If it is found that the savings do not compensate for the inconvenience caused the matter will be looked at again.

Yours etc.
Councillor Robert Naismith.'

'Dear Sir,

In my humble opinion Miss Jennifer Kerr should think black burning shame of herself. Everyone in Lunderston knows that she has never worked or wanted. We are not all so lucky as to be left a fortune by our fathers. Living in her big villa by the sea-front, she has the audacity to say that £35 a week is an exorbitant sum for keeping two lavatories clean. I challenge her to put in the first offer for the Ardpatrick lavatories. If she thinks privatisation such a good idea why doesn't she grab some of the profits? I have no doubt she is perfectly willing to spend billions of pounds on Trident, which will benefit nobody, and yet she grudges spending a few pounds on facilities that, as previous letters have shown, are a necessity to many people.

> Yours sincerely,
> Mary McClure
> 12 The Glebe.'

'Dear Sir,

It never ceases to amuse me the way Scottish Nationalists get in their propaganda. Mr Malcolm McPherson was too shy, or was it too sly? to disclose in his letter that he is President of the Lunderston branch of that Party. How can he say that it is the Parliament in London that has closed our lavatories? This has been done by order of a Council consisting entirely of Scotsmen. How could we manage a country when we cannot manage our public lavatories?

> Yours faithfully,
> Dick Reid
> 61 Carrick Avenue.'

'Dear Sir,

Having read Mr Alec Sproat's heart-rending letter in last week's issue, I would like to ask, as discreetly as I can, what would have happened had he, unable through infirmity to contain himself, relieved himself against the wall of the closed lavatory? Would he have been arrested for indecency?

Let me recount something that I saw with my own eyes. It was at Ibrox Stadium, home of Glasgow Rangers, some years ago. Just before half-time one of the spectators went to relieve himself against the wall that surrounds the ground. Immediately a policeman appeared and threatened him with arrest for, I suppose, indecent behaviour. I was too far off to hear what was said. While the culprit was expostulating – his gestures indicated that that was what he was doing – the half-time whistle blew and immediately instead of one there were literally hundreds making use of that wall. The policeman, much crestfallen, was glad to creep away. Of course the trouble was that there were not enough lavatories. Here in Lunderston we have enough but the Council in its foolishness has closed most of them.

Yours sincerely,
Ian Maxwell
55 Springfield Drive.'

'Dear Sir,

The correspondence in your newspaper about the padlocking of lavatories in Lunderston has set me thinking. How is it that we are being constantly told that as a nation we are more prosperous than ever before, and yet we can see for ourselves that the quality of life has declined? Our Victorian ancestors built our public lavatories to last, knowing that there would always be a need for them. Now we find them locked in our faces. There was a time in living memory when the Firth of Clyde was crowded with pleasure boats which had bands on board and restaurants with white cloths on the tables. Now there are only drab utilitarian car ferries. Old Lunderstonians will tell you that it was once possible to be driven in a horse carriage from the pier to Ardpatrick Point. Gracious living indeed! Once you could have your luggage carried by porters, and your newspaper delivered to your door. Once there were recitals of music almost every evening in summer in the public park. Once everybody in the town who was fit rambled along the promenade on Sunday evenings after the kirks skailed, chatting to friends. Once there were six boat-hirers, today there is only one. We shut ourselves off from one another in little tin boxes on wheels or sit at home watching Transatlantic rubbish on television. We have not only put padlocks on our lavatories, we have put them on our souls too.

Yours,
Donald Colquhoun,
"Toward View" East Bay.'

By the following week the Council had changed its mind. The lavatories were to be closed only during the winter months. The correspondence therefore, in the editor's opinion, was no longer necessary. Nevertheless in the interests of fairness he published two more letters.

'Dear Sir,

Like many others of your readers I enjoyed Mr Donald Colquhoun's eloquent letter in your last issue, and in many respects find myself in agreement with him. I would like to point out however that the reason why there were so many pleasure steamers, and porters, and boys delivering newspapers, was that wages then were so scandalously low. Those lucky enough to be comfortably off were, whether or not intentionally, exploiting those less fortunate. People then living in villas on the sea-front, such as Mr Colquhoun's, in those days employed a servant, sometimes two, because these were paid pittances. Today, when domestic servants expect to be paid a reasonable wage, there is no demand for their services.

As for the closing of the lavatories, I wonder if this is legal? Are not local authorities required by statute to provide such amenities? This all comes from having Cabinet Ministers who never travel on buses or trains or use public lavatories. How then can they know how ordinary people live?

Yours faithfully,
James Gibson,
4 Sannox Road.'

'Dear Sir,

Writing on behalf of the ladies of St Cuthbert's Women's Guild, I wish to complain in the strongest terms about the correspondence going on at present in your newspaper. We consider it vulgar and disgusting. It appeals to the degraded elements in our town. They consider it a subject for indecent jests, which are to be heard everywhere. We, with young children to bring up, are not amused. Please publish no more letters on this subject.

Yours sincerely
Moira McFadyen (Mrs)
President, St Cuthbert's Women's Guild.'

The Book Club

WHEN THE AMERICAN AIR BASE was first set up, a few miles out of town, half a dozen Lunderston ladies who liked reading thought it would be a good idea to seek out six similarly minded American ladies and form a book club. It would be a hospitable gesture and would contribute towards establishing a friendly relationship between the incomers and the natives. They would meet every fortnight in one another's houses and discuss a book previously agreed upon. It would inevitably be a middle-class affair, the Scottish ladies being the wives or widows of business men, school teachers, or civil servants, while the American ladies' husbands were all officers.

Thanks to the determination of the Scottish ladies the idea became a reality.

The houses where they met were, on the Scottish side, owner-occupied, semi-detached or detached villas in residential areas. Most of the American ladies lived in a small estate specially built for officers and their families about two miles out of town, but some preferred to rent houses in Lunderston itself, to be near shops and schools, and also, it was suspected, to be apart from their compatriots.

From the beginning there was a disparity in the ages of the two sections. The Americans, wives of lieutenants, were a good deal younger than the Scots, who were all middle-aged. The Americans' children were toddlers, those of the Scots university students. This imbalance, it was realised, would get worse, for the Americans had to be changed every three years while the Scots remained fixtures. What it amounted to was that the American ladies remained at the same age, while the Scots got older. This could not help but cause complications.

When it was the turn of an American lady to entertain the club she might have to excuse herself to go off and put Junior on his pot or suckle Baby. The Scottish ladies were tolerant but in their hearts not pleased, in their houses only the dog or cat interrupted the literary discussion. Still, they had had their day of wiping bottoms and suckling, so they were happy to make allowances.

Sometimes the books proposed by one side were not to the taste of the other. An account of some young American woman's sexual misadventures, delivered in a scatty headlong conversational style, was as remote from the Scottish ladies' experience as the habits of the Inuits of North Canada. They would listen in polite stupefaction to enthusiastic, or even ecstatic, praises of this frothy nonsense, and when it came to their turn to express their opinion they did so diplomatically. At least five of them did. Isabel Shivas could never be depended on to be discreet.

The loquacity of some of the young Americans was a sore trial to the Scots. It was in such contrast to their own canny terseness. They would stare at their shoes as first one, from Louisiana, say, and then another, from Minnesota, blethered at great length and with gushing zest, about nothing at all.

It was tacitly agreed that politics were to be avoided. On one famous occasion an American lady rather guilelessly remarked that she and her sister expatriates were giving up all the benefits and amenities of home in order to protect

Britain and Europe from the wicked Russians, and yet they
were given no credit for it. It had been too much for Isabel.
She had retorted bluntly that the Americans were in Britain
and Europe to defend their own homeland from as far away
as possible, so that if war occurred no bombs would fall on
it, in the same way that no bombs had fallen on it during the
last war. None of the Americans had contradicted her, none
of the Scots had supported her. Her words had lain among
them like an unexploded bomb, not only then but for years
afterwards.

It wasn't that she was a Bolshevik or anything like that. On
the contrary, she was the best-off of them all, including the
Americans. A widow, whose husband had made a fortune in
South Africa, she lived by herself in one of the biggest houses
in Lunderston. Small, stout, and imperious, she reminded
her friends of Queen Victoria, and she was just as often not
amused. She had a son and daughter, both married, still in
South Africa, and sometimes visited them. Indeed, she was
an intrepid traveller. With a woman friend about her own
age, at that time sixty or so, she had gone to Russia, China,
and Cuba, to find out if the egalitarians were as equal as they
claimed. Her verdict was that they were not. She had also
been to India and Brazil. Of the former she had said that
vasectomies ought to be compulsory, and of the latter that
the Pope, who had been there the year before her, ought to
be ashamed of himself. 'All those hungry unwanted children.'
In St Cuthbert's it was said that Mr Henderson the minister
always looked apprehensively at the place where she always
sat. If he saw her there his sermon of cosy platitudes was never
delivered as confidently as when she was absent. Sometimes
she would skip a meeting of the book club. 'If it's at that
silly fat creature's, no thanks.' When she did turn up, in a
big BMW that had belonged to her husband, her arrival was
watched from the window with anxiety. She parked her car

by bumping other cars out of the way. Offers of lifts were haughtily rejected. Had they not noticed that she had a car of her own, a better one than theirs? As she got older her arthritis got worse, so did her temper. Her Scottish colleagues in the club talked among themselves about coaxing her to resign, but none was bold enough to put it to her. In any case, she would have been missed. She kept them in suspense, like a good book.

Twenty-seven years after its inception the book club was wound up. Interest had waned. Seldom more than six attended. The Scots contingent, all white-haired, was reduced to four, one having died, and another being in hospital dying. The young Americans were busy with their own purely American affairs or else they were visiting other parts of Europe. It was agreed therefore, with regret but also with relief, that the time had come to declare the book club at an end. There was to be a farewell lunch. The Americans suggested Knelin Castle, three miles out of town and very expensive. The Scots felt it should be in Lunderston, in the Royal Hotel, say, which was not quite so dear, though the food was just as good. The Americans good-humouredly agreed. The cost would be £15 each, which would include a pre-lunch cocktail and two bottles of wine. Everybody thought that reasonable, except Isabel. 'A ridiculous price' she said. 'What are we trying to do? Show-off? Why not the Eldorado?' This was a fast-food cafe frequented by teen-agers; it had a juke-box. They knew she was just being difficult, but she was now seventy-five and hirpled, with the help of a stick. She still drove a car, however, a small Mini now, and every other motorist in Lunderston kept well out of her way.

The American ladies were so eager to have a full turnout that one of them cut short a holiday in Italy to be back in time.

Except perhaps for one the present batch of Americans were pleasant, obliging, and intelligent young women, most respectful to their elderly Scottish counterparts. The exception was a 'girner' from Virginia. The word was Isabel's. Whatever the book chosen Celestine made it a vehicle for personal complaints about her health, her children's health, her husband's lack of promotion (he was a dentist) and the Scottish climate, which was always spoiling outings that she and her family had planned. She was harmless, however, a squeaky mouse compared to Isabel's glowering cat. She and Isabel had encounters now and then, but the latter's claws had been kept sheathed.

The day of the lunch was a Tuesday in May. The sun shone, the Firth sparkled. As the ladies gathered on the terrace of the Royal Hotel, drinking their sherries or cocktails or Coca-Colas, they chatted about this or that, waiting for the two latecomers, Celestine and Isabel. They were often late, the former because of the disorganised way she lived, the latter out of mischievous deliberation. The others, though none said so, would have been pleased if neither of them showed up. They did not want the occasion spoiled by Celestine's girns or Isabel's rudeness. Her friends too were afraid that Isabel, who couldn't be bothered dressing up nowadays, would be wearing the clothes she did her housework in.

They were pleasantly surprised. A taxi came up the drive and out of it climbed, with difficulty, a resplendent Isabel. She was wearing a red dress of lustrous stuff that though old-fashioned and smelling of mothballs would have suited a duchess, and pearls and rings that would have made any duchess envious. She had her white hair blue rinsed, and on her feet, usually shod in bauchles, were shoes of the finest quality, though hardly fashionable. Even so, they all hesitated to run out and help her. In spite of her finery she was still likely to give them raps with her stick for interfering. The stick itself was not the usual gnarled hickory but elegant mahogany, with round it bands of silver.

They were still not altogether reassured. Was this Isabel in war paint?

Minutes later came a telephone call from Celestine. She was sorry, hysterically so, but she would not be able to come. Wayne Junior had been up all night sick. 'Greedy little pig,' said Isabel, amiably enough. The doctor had been and given him medicine but he was still very pale. She had to stay home and look after him. She understood that her money was not refundable though it was rather unfair since how could any mother tell when her child of five was going to be sick? 'If she sees him stuffing himself with junk she should be able to tell,' was Isabel's restrained comment. She had chosen Glenmorangie as an aperitif.

They had a special room of their own, with a big bow window giving a view of the sunny Firth.

A toast was proposed: To all members of the Book Club, past and present.

'One is dead,' observed Isabel. 'Is it in order to toast a dead person?' But she joined in, and said nothing when two of the Americans drank the toast in Coca-Cola. She contented herself with a frown.

An American, known for her exuberance, suggested toasting the Queen and the President.

'Why not Mr Gorbachev too?' asked Isabel.

The idea was dropped.

The Scottish ladies wondered what Isabel was up to. Usually when she shot down flighty ideas she did it grimly. Today she was doing it with a smile. It came to the same thing of course. But was she waiting for her chance to go off, like that unexploded bomb? They kept their fingers crossed.

She decided that two bottles of wine weren't enough, so

she ordered two more. 'It's all right,' she said, to the faces turned reproachfully at her. 'I'll pay.'

'It's not that, Isabel. They're not needed. Cynthia and Marlene aren't drinking wine.'

'That's their misfortune. All the more for the rest of us.'

'Have you forgotten, we're driving?'

'Take a taxi. Pick up your cars tomorrow.'

'But, Isabel – '

'Do what you like, I don't care.'

The excellence of the food encouraged them to drink the extra wine, though they did it sheepishly and guiltily.

In the midst of the chatter Isabel proposed a minute's silence for Lizzie McPhail, dead of cancer, and Jean Hislop in hospital dying of it.

Though some of them suspected her motives were not pure they were all in favour. Some shed tears during the minute of remembrance. The Scots ladies wondered which of them would be next to go. Opening their eyes to glance at Isabel, they were sure it wouldn't be her. That contemptuous smile, they knew, wasn't for them or their two friends, one dead and the other dying, but for death itself. She had once embarrassed them all and shocked some of the Americans by declaring that she did not believe in an after-life. Death could not be cheated but it could be outfaced.

Everyone then was called on to provide an anecdote connected with the club.

They had all something to tell.

There was the day in January a few years ago when the rendezvous was up Glen Kin, where Helga Gottlieb and her husband had rented a cottage. During the two-and-a-half hours discussion – the book, an epic of nine hundred pages, had provoked passionate disagreements – snow had fallen steadily and blocked the road. A snow-plough had had to clear it before they could get home, four hours late.

There had been the book unwittingly and naively proposed by Eugenie Yandell. It had been full of four letter words and scenes of explicit sex. Some had refused to read beyond the first two pages.

'I think I was the only one to speak in its favour,' said Isabel.

'So you were, Isabel, and we still don't know why.'

'You said some terrible things, Isabel, if I remember rightly.'

'I remember saying that I agreed with the author's insinuation that so-called respectable ladies, such as ourselves, were more interested in sex than they would ever admit.'

It was recalled that Lizzie McPhail wouldn't read a book written in the first person.

'Which was odd,' said Isabel, 'considering that she was always talking about herself.'

'Poor Lizzie, she's not talking about herself now.'

'That, Janet, is a very silly thing to say.'

There had been Candice Wirtenheim who had telephoned from Rome at twelve o'clock to give her opinion of the book the club was then discussing.

'What she really wanted to do,' said Isabel, 'was to let us know what a marvellous holiday she was having. But then she was always talking about herself. Like Lizzie. But not for the same reason. Well, not exactly for the same reason. Lizzie just liked to show off, but Mrs W. did it because she was in search of her true identity. So at least did she inform us, frequently.'

'But, Isabel, aren't we all in search of our true identity? From the cradle to the grave.'

'Didn't you go to Russia and China in search of yours?'

'I went to find out about other people. I have never made the mistake of carrying my prejudices about with me.'

There were gasps at that.

Someone then recalled the time when they had gathered round Zoe Salter's bed as she was nursing Hiram Edward, recently born.

To everyone's amazement and relief Isabel, sipping brandy, offered no comment.

She asked to be kept to the last. When it was her turn they waited as apprehensively as Mr Henderson in his pulpit. They had no idea what she would say. Perhaps she had been storing up anti-American prejudice and would now let it all pour out. They noticed how contorted her hands were with arthritis. She could scarcely hold the brandy glass. If she delivered a bitter diatribe against the Americans or rather against their President whom she had often called a fool, her real targets would be old age, decrepitude, and pain.

'I'd just like to say a word in praise of books.'

They sighed with relief but still waited with foreboding.

'They have given us a great deal of pleasure.'

'Hear, hear, Isabel.'

'Even the most rubbishy books give pleasure to lots of people. They may not be the most intelligent people in the world, but that's not their fault, nor is it their misfortune. I have often noticed that the stupidest people are usually the happiest. What could be more contented than a cow in a field on a sunny day?' She smiled.

It was risky enough trying to interpret her words without taking on her smile as well.

'Often we read a book without bothering to look at the author's name. That has always struck me as most ungrateful.'

'How very true, Isabel.'

'So if you'll allow me I would like, on behalf of our book club, now defunct, to thank all authors, whether we liked their books or not.'

'Of course, Isabel.'

'Thank you for reminding us, Isabel.'

'A toast to the authors!'

Solemnly the toast was drunk.

Perhaps one or two of the Americans wondered if her remark about rubbishly books had been directed at those of them who had recommended books dismissed by her at the time as rubbish, but if so surely what she had just said was a kind of apology.

At the finish there was a confusion of shaking hands and kissing cheeks and promising to keep in touch. One rather tipsy American was about to propose that they sing 'Old Lang Zyne', but a glance at Isabel's face warned her not to. Isabel in her charity might give praise to the authors of rubbishly books but she was damned if she was going to act like a character in one of them.

The Ladies' Section

GOLFERS WILL TELL YOU that what is most important
in the playing of their game – though they would insist
that it is more than a game – is not skill in smiting a small
ball, but probity. In other games, such as tennis and football,
cheating is difficult, for your opponents or the referee or the
spectators will catch you out and therefore not to cheat is
hardly meritorious, but in golf, a more private and lonelier
game, it is all left to your own conscience. Your opponent
or playing partner is in honour bound not to rush across and
overlook suspiciously what you are up to when your ball has
landed in a thicket of whin or clump of heather. If you cheat
by moving the ball to a spot where it can more easily be
reached by your club and by not declaring that you have
done so, there is no way by which you can be found out and
accused. This is not to say that golfers never cheat. A few do
and lie awake at night with lacerated consciences. They are
always found out in the end. Their furtiveness gives them
away. Expelled from the club, and from the freemasonry of
golfers, they are broken men, with no purpose left in life.

Off the course, alas, golfers are not such paragons. They
have the same shortcomings as ordinary men. In one respect
they show themselves to be inferior to or meaner-minded
than, for example, bowlers. From the very beginning they

have been churlish about letting women join in. They have given various reasons, none of them completely honest.

Swinging a golf club, they say, is not a natural physical action. Even the most skilful professional, whose swing looks so smooth and rhythmical, is subjecting the muscles of his back, not to mention his spine, to exceptional stress and strain. Men's bodies can stand a good deal of this before breaking down, but even so many golfers have bad backs. Women's bodies being weaker and softer would soon break down. Either that or they would become muscular and tough, which would please neither themselves nor their husbands. Therefore they should be prevented from playing golf, for their own good.

Golf takes up a great deal of time. Women have neither the temperament nor the patience for it. Besides, how could they run their households competently if they spent three hours or more on a golf course?

Through no fault of their own, for they are as God made them, women lack imagination. They are literal-minded. They see golf as simply a pastime. For them it has no mystical connotations. In the clubhouse, where men discuss esoteric aspects with the devotion of priests, women with their shrill chatter about extraneous things like children and the price of beef would be like infidels in a church.

The most honest reason is usually kept to the last. A golf course is a place for men, just as tournament lists were in ancient days. Men do not seek to enter sewing circles. Women ought to show the same tact and good sense by keeping off golf courses.

For many years, indeed for centuries, women were resolutely excluded. Even today a few clubs have still not yielded. Most, however, have had to give in, in many cases not very graciously.

*   *   *

Lunderston Golf Club was founded in 1890 by a group of knickerbockered devotees, all men of substance in the town. Since there were no stretches of sandy links as at Troon they had to rent some hilly fields from a farmer and share them with his sheep and cattle. Greens were makeshift and had to be protected with barbed wire, low enough for golfers to step over without tearing their stockings, but high enough to discourage sheep, whose droppings would have made putting impossible. Cowpats were numerous. A local rule had to be introduced, according to which a ball that landed in one could be lifted, cleaned, and replaced, without penalty. Several similar local rules were necessary, to be added to the body of regulations drawn up by the Royal and Ancient Club of St Andrews. There were only ten holes at first, resourcefully laid out. A stone hut was rented from the farmer and used as a clubhouse. It was really only a shelter from the rain, with nothing to sit on but cans that had once contained sheep-dip. When there was no rain and the sun shone the views of the Firth and the islands were splendid.

At that time there was no danger of women intruding. Their long skirts would have got muddied and drenched, or ripped by the thorns of whins and brambles. They preferred to meet in the tearooms and laugh at their men's foolishness. So it never occurred to those early golfers of Lunderston, as they expended money and effort on improving their course and building a clubhouse, that these would one day be invaded by their daughters and grand-daughters.

During the First World War the course was given up to the cows and sheep. Parts of it were ploughed up to produce food. The wooden clubhouse fell into disrepair. Older members did not think it right that they should play golf while their young colleagues were dying in France, but some of them on sunny days walked over what was left of the course, swiping off the heads of thistles, as a way of keeping the memory of the game alive.

After the war there was an influx of members. Artisans of the town, young men who had come back from the trenches to claim their rights, applied to join and could hardly be denied, since after all they had helped to save the country from the Huns. They proved excellent members. Eager to improve their social status, they willingly accepted all the rules about dress, deportment, and etiquette. Their keenness to win raised standards of play, though some of the original members grumbled that there was now too much emphasis on competitions and the old days of playing for the fun of it were gone for good. Above all, the young lions were found to be even more stoutly opposed to women membership than the old bears had ever been. The place for women, they said, was in the home, and their wives meekly acquiesced.

It was different however with the ladies who lived in the villas along the sea-front or in the mansions up in Ailsa Park. They had plenty of leisure and read magazines in which appeared photographs of lady golfers, some of them titled. Led by Mrs Scrimgeour, whose husband happened to be Club Captain that year, they banded together in 1924 and wrote a letter to the Committee, demanding that the question of allowing ladies to become members be considered forthwith. It was received with horror and anger. There was no debate. Not one member of the Committee was in favour. The letter notifying the ladies of the decision was short but firm. It stated that the Committee was unanimously of the opinion that golf was not a suitable game for ladies. Much incensed, the ladies sent another letter in which they challenged the Committee to put so important a matter to the entire membership at the next annual general meeting. Mr Scrimgeour, bullied it was suspected by his wife, argued that it would do no harm to have the matter discussed and dismissed once and for all. When the ladies saw how total was the opposition to their membership they would drop the idea. This was reluctantly agreed to. Mrs Scrimgeour and Mrs Turriff, wife of a bank manager, were to be permitted to address the assembled membership briefly, putting their case.

There were at that time 155 members, far too many for the clubhouse to accommodate, if they all came, and all were determined to come, to show solidarity in face of this threat of female intrusion. Also there were no toilet facilities for women. Therefore the meeting was held in the Temperance Hall, where no alcoholic refreshments could be had, but there were several public houses within easy distance, and many members dropped into these on their way to the meeting. They intended to drop into them again after it, this time to celebrate the rout of the hussies.

With the members of the Committee on the platform, under a Rechabitic banner, and with John Scrimgeour as Chairman, lesser matters were quickly got out of the way, until they came to the outstanding issue of the evening: not the question of female membership, but whether or not the club should purchase Toward View Hotel, which was adjacent to the course and would make an admirable clubhouse. The burgh had promised help with a loan at a low rate of interest, but unfortunately it would still mean a sharp rise in the annual subscription. What were needed, said the Chairman, were philanthropic members to lend the club, interest-free, fifty pounds (quite a considerable sum in those days) or better still to make it a gift of that amount. He offered himself as the first such benefactor, and in a very short time, for such was the enthusiasm, thirty-two followed his example. There was much applause. The motion that the club should purchase Toward View Hotel ('those who come after us will bless our memory') was carried by acclaim. Everybody was excited. The future of golf in Lunderston was assured. They would be the envy of other clubs.

It was an anti-climax when the Chairman called them to order and reminded them that there still remained one more item of business. (Members groaned.) If no one objected he would at once call on the two ladies to state their case.

Objections were being shouted when the two ladies came on to the platform, annoyed at having been kept waiting so long. They thought, unjustly, that it had been a deliberate ploy, in order to make them lose heart. As a consequence they urged their case more peevishly than was prudent and did not forego sarcasm.

Mrs Scrimgeour, a large lady with a dominant voice, at once began to read out a list of golf clubs which had, as she put it, moved with the times, and admitted lady members. None of them had regretted it. On the contrary all acknowledged that the social life of their club had been greatly improved. Left to themselves men were inclined to be uncivilised. Women had a broader vision and a softer touch. They would make the clubhouse a haven of comfort and elegance. (Groans and shouts of dissent.) As for lady golfers, were they aware that a certain woman professional regularly hit the ball 250 yards? Who in that hall could do as well? Given the chance, women would quickly show they were as proficient as men. (Shouts of outrage.) Not being as strong as men, they would make up for it by accuracy and delicacy of touch. Then, provoked by the many jeers, she made a disclosure which she knew would infuriate them, but she could not resist it. 'As you all know, gentlemen, par for the course is seventy-one. The present record stands at sixty-seven. Well, this very summer, at six o'clock one sunny Sunday morning, while you were all asleep, Miss Zoe Tubinski, an American, whom you will probably have heard of, accompanied by myself and Mrs Turriff as witnesses, played a round over the course and returned a score of sixty-eight. I have her card here authenticated by myself and Mrs Turriff.' She held it up, not, alas, to cheers but to scandalised boos.

It wasn't so much that they disbelieved her though they did, it was the sheer deceitfulness of inviting, behind their backs, a female professional, an American at that, to play on their course, without permission. It was an act of sacrilege no less and the damned woman was proud of it. No wonder the Chairman, her husband, looked sick. It had long been suspected and was now proved that he was under her domination.

All over the hall men were jumping to their feet and shouting protests. It was only after many anguished appeals that the Chairman was able to restore order. 'Let us remember, gentlemen, that however provoked we are still gentlemen. As golfers we have a reputation for fair play. The ladies are prepared to answer questions. I beg that these be relevant and courteous.'

The first question was 'What did it cost you to bring her all the way to Lunderston?'

'What Miss Tubinski was paid is no concern of yours, sir.'

'By how much was the course shortened for her benefit?'

'Miss Tubinski played off those tees with white markers.'

There were howls of incredulity. Those were the medal tees, used by the men only in competitions. Even if, God forbid, women were one day allowed they would be made to use tees at least fifty yards ahead of the men's ordinary tees, in recognition of their inferior strength (they weren't all brawny like Zoe Tubinski) but more importantly to prevent their comparing their scores with those of men. If a woman was to come in with a net score of seventy-five, say, and wanted to crow over a man who had scored a net seventy-eight, he must be able to point out that she had been playing a shorter and easier course than he. That was how it was done in those weak-kneed clubs which had let women in. The men there had to be vigilant lest their pride as golfers, which was the same as their pride as men, was made ridiculous by some female Goliath. It must never happen at Lunderston.

At last the ladies withdrew and the vote was taken. To everyone's astonishment it was not unanimous. Twenty-five voted in favour of the women. The traitors themselves were astonished. They had not meant, when they had entered the hall, to support the women. Asked for an explanation, all they could mumble was 'It's bound to come one day, we all know that.' 'Over our dead bodies,' cried the majority, prophetically, it turned out, in quite a few cases.

Twenty-six years later the women of Lunderston were at last successful. Though victory was sullenly conceded they did not have to put up as hard a fight as their defeated predecessors. Circumstances were more propitious. Another World War had just been fought in which women had played a useful and courageous part. They now had leisure for activities outside the home, since they no longer went in for large families. Their skirts were not now of inconvenient length and the war had accustomed them to wearing trousers. Even the most misogynistic of golfers had no answer but a baffled snarl when it was pointed out to them how unjust it was that men from neighbouring towns and even from distant Glasgow were accepted as members while women born and bred in the town were barred. None the less the majority in favour was not large, and even the few enthusiastic about admitting the ladies agreed that they could not possibly be granted the same rights and conditions as men. They were to play off their own forward tees. They must not take part in men's competitions. They must keep off the course on Saturdays and Sundays before three pm. They had no voting rights and were not entitled to be represented on the Committee. The names of lady captains and champions were not to be put up in gold letters on the board in the hall, like those of male captains and champions. Above all, they must not at any time come into the big lounge, which had the best views from its windows and the most comfortable chairs. These were humiliating restrictions, but the women, who numbered only fifteen at the beginning, had to put up with them. The time would come, said the optimists among them, when they would be on an equal footing with the men, but even those who said it did not believe it.

Twenty years later those restrictions were still in force. The original fifteen had increased by only five, and most were now middle-aged or elderly. This meant that young girls who might have been interested in taking up golf were discouraged by having to associate with women whose attitudes on and off the course were old-fashioned. Also they could not accept being treated by the men as pariahs. They came once or twice, objected to being herded into a corner and to being there on sufferance, and so gave up. Chauvinists among the men were pleased. They happily foresaw a time when the unwelcome band would have dwindled to only two or three white-haired arthritic old diehards, and then to none at all. But that was before the advent of Kate Merrilees.

She came from the north-east to be Principal Teacher of Physical Education in Lunderston Academy. Her appointment was noted with interest in the men's lounge at the golf club, for she happened to be the reigning amateur ladies' champion of Scotland and had done well in Great Britain's Curtis Cup team against the Americans. If she joined Lunderston, and the secretary had already had a letter from her, she would bring distinction to the club but she might also cause alarm by the quality of her play. Would she be as good as, or even better than, the club's champion? As for the men in Division One, with handicaps of eight and under, who were very proud of their prowess and worked hard to improve it, they might well be outshone by her, and though one or two would take it sportingly most would be chagrined. Indeed, one was heard muttering into his beer that he would give up the game rather than be put to shame by a woman, even if she was good-looking. For Miss Merrilees was not only an excellent golfer, she was also handsome and athletic, judging from her appearances on television.

As for the rabbits, those with handicaps of twenty and over, they were scared by the prospect of this greyhound coming amongst them.

She came, one Tuesday, the day the ladies held their competitions, and introduced herself. It would have been extravagant to liken them to a band of ageing Amazons disheartened by many defeats suddenly confronted by the goddess Diana come to succour them, but they were certainly uplifted and afterwards held their heads high. Perhaps they were a little uneasy at Miss Merrilees' pushy manner and they listened with foreboding to her zestful talk of recruiting senior girls for the club and so expanding and revitalising the Ladies Section, but she was none the less a godsend and they rejoiced.

The first time she played over the course was a sunny Saturday afternoon. It was a friendly game with the club's hitherto best lady golfers, Mrs Kirkwood and Miss McCulloch. She was tastefully turned out, in yellow slacks and a white pullover which had the British Curtis Cup badge on it. From the windows of their special reserve men watched her practice swings and were grudgingly impressed by the graceful vigour she put into them. Discussing her previously, they had agreed that judged by men's standards she would be ranked as second-class, but seeing her now in action they had to admit that not many second-class or for that matter first-class golfers swung a club so smoothly and lithely. All right, she had style, but everybody knew that swinging in practice was a very different thing from swinging in earnest. Forgetting to drink their beers and whiskies, they waited for her to drive off.

On the first tee the ladies' marker was only a few yards ahead of the men's, so she was being given a negligible advantage. At that first hole there was an old quarry covered with whin bushes about 150 yards from the tee. Most ladies' drives fell short of this, and many men's too. Some men drove into it and as often as not lost their balls. Only the top players could hit their balls over it. The present club champion, Steve Livingstone, a big beefy young man of twenty-two, had been known to send his a good 100 yards beyond. How would Miss Merrilees' compare with *that*? Yet Steve was never likely to be known outside Lunderston. There were in the county, still more in the whole country, men as good as he or better, who still would never be famous nationally, far less internationally, as Miss Merrilees was. This showed, did it not, the great gulf between men's standards and women's? Thus they cogitated as they watched her prepare to drive. They knew that in driving it was timing that counted most, not brute force, but brute force could add on some 20 or 30 yards. Miss Merrilees had not much brute force and Steve Livingstone had a great deal. Yet to their amazement there was her ball soaring over the quarry and landing in the same area where Steve's best efforts landed. With reluctant admiration and much disquiet they watched her shoulder her bag and stride off up the fairway, while her two partners, who had both hit respectable drives almost to the quarry, pulled their trolleys behind them. Something had happened to the club. Whether it was a good thing or a bad thing could not yet be told. When a goddess appeared among mortals were they benefited or harmed?

Some three hours later, from the windows that overlooked

the eighteenth green, some of the same men, and others who had come later into the clubhouse, watched as Miss Merrilees approached. No attention was paid to her two companions, although they, profiting from her example and tuition, had done a lot better than usual and were very pleased with themselves. Was Miss Merrilees, wondered the watchers at the windows, about to hit her second or third shot? If her second then she must have hit a tremendous drive indeed. That hole was a long par four of 460 yards for men and about 40 yards less for women. Even so, for her ball to be where it now was, about 180 yards from the hole, was incredible. They watched as she addressed and then struck the ball, smoothly, without strain. In disbelief they saw it alight in front of the green and run on until it came to rest no more than five yards from the hole. She would be putting for a birdie three, if, that was, they were right in their count. Not many players could manage par fours at that hole, and threes were very rare.

At last all three players were on the green. Some ladies watching from their own small lounge must have asked by signs how many strokes Miss Merrilees had taken to get to where she was. Mrs Kirkwood held up two fingers. So Miss Merrilees was putting for a three. She went about it briskly. There was no crouching or squatting or squinting or prowling, She took a good look and then crisply tapped the ball. Everybody, including herself, was sure that it was going to drop into the hole, but, travelling a shade too fast, it jumped over, coming to rest six inches away. It was a fine putt, and she was entitled to feel cheated. No one would have blamed her if she had scowled with disappointment. But no, she laughed, and cordially shook hands with her playing partners. As a golfer she could not be faulted, nor as a woman either, for as she bent to pick up her bag she showed a neat shapely bottom. Someone stole out to find what her score for the round had been. He soon came back, his face a mixture of dolefulness and delight. Miss Merrilees, he reported, had been round in seventy.

Four of the older members, all of them over sixty, sat in their favourite corner, drinking whisky and discussing Miss Merrilees and her likely effect on the club.

'The writing's on the wall,' said Jack Crawford. 'We're the dinosaurs now. Time for us to become extinct.'

His friends grinned. Jack had always been in the forefront of those opposed to women members.

'You're laughing,' he said, 'but the Committee will have my resignation on Monday.'

'Isn't that a bit hasty, Jack?' asked Bob Logan.

'Not to say drastic,' said Archie Cooper.

'Especially when your subscription's valid till the end of the year,' said Jim McLaughlin, cannily.

'What we've just seen's only the beginning,' said Jack. 'I'm not going to be here when they take over.'

They saw what he meant. Because of Miss Merrilees lots of women would take an interest in golf and want to join the club, some of them mere schoolgirls, well able to hit a ball further than old men of sixty-five. It would be intolerable to have one's decrepitude shown up in such a fashion. Yet how could the aches and miseries of old age be endured without the consolations of golf, even when played shakily?

'They can't take us over, Jack,' said Archie. 'They're outnumbered, by ten to one.'

'Just you wait. That woman will have dozens of them joining.'

'The Committee wouldn't allow it,' said Bob.

'The other ladies wouldn't like it,' said Jim.

'You're forgetting, that woman's famous. She's been seen on television. They'll not be able to say no to her. I've seen it coming. You all laughed at me. Who's laughing now? Who's our present champion?'

'Steve Livingstone.'

'Right. I can't say I like his manners on the course, winning's everything with him, but suppose she was to play him and beat him, where would we all be then?'

'She could never beat him,' said Archie, uneasily.

'Anyway, they'll never play in the same competitions,' said Bob.

'What if those damned women challenged our champion to play theirs?'

One of those damned women was Jim McLaughlin's wife. 'That's a thing they're likely to do,' he said, 'now that they've got Miss Merrilees.'

'Would it be so terrible,' asked Bob, 'if the best player in the club was a woman? After all, Jack, we've got a woman Prime Minister whom you think's marvellous.'

'That's different.'

They looked at one another and nodded. Yes, that was different. It didn't affect them nearly as intimately as women running the golf club would.

'She'll get up a competition,' said Jack, 'to be played here at Lunderston. She'll call it the Lunderston Cup. She'll invite all the lady champions to play in it. We'll see slips of girls hit past the quarry or reach the green at the twelfth. The course will be desecrated.'

Was that really the word? Wasn't it a bit strong? No. Remembering what golf meant to them, they realised that Jack was right. Out on that course, bright now in the evening sunshine, were many favourite spots, which could almost be called shrines. The birches behind the fourteenth green, where deer lurked. The copse of rowans to the left of the twelfth fairway, glorious first with their white flourish and then their red berries. The burn that crossed the thirteenth

119

fairway, where, if your ball landed in it, it disturbed trout. The ruins near the seventh green, said to be those of an ancient castle. The rhododendrons everywhere. From all those places and others the presence of too many women would take away the holiness. They would not mean to do it, they would indignantly deny that they were doing it, but they would do it all the same.

These were fears too deep and mysterious to be spoken. The four elderly men sipped their whisky and shuddered.

The Consultant

F OR MANY YEARS BILLY McShane was one of the most
controversial figures in Lunderston. Probably no one
outside his family circle – a large group, for he was married
twice, with ten children by his first wife and eight by his second
– loved him, many despised him as a workshy scrounger, a few
pitied him for he claimed to have a weak heart which prevented
him from working, and one or two admired his grasp of social
security regulations. Most Lunderstonians, as they watched him
paddling his canoe, as it were, past many rocky waterfalls, with
only one serious mishap, gave him some grudged respect but
few wished him well. His morality was too unorthodox, his
appearance too unprepossessing, though to be fair his red face
and big purple nose were not caused by drink, nor was his
wheezing caused by smoking, nor his stoutness by gluttony.
If to smile amiably at detractors and refrain from defending
yourself with retaliatory abuse, is an indication of moral courage
and Christian forbearance then Billy often showed that he had
those rare qualities in abundance. If to be patient and loving
towards your children, when you have two howling in the pram
and another clinging to your legs, proved you a model father,
then Billy proved it every day, not in back streets either where
no one would sneer at his subsidised paternity but in the main
street, among the contemptuous crowds.

If he had cringed or whined a little he would have been more readily forgiven, but no, he held up his head in any company and made his many demands on the State frankly, as if he was doing it a good turn by giving it opportunities to be caring and compassionate. Exaggerated tales were told of the concessions he had screwed out of the authorities: bedding, clothes, perambulators, first-communion dresses for his daughters, a washing-machine, and a coloured television set. It was said that in the supermarket he was seen to pull out a wad of notes to pay for his trolleyful of purchases, among which, it was claimed, were bars of chocolate and bottles of wine. What was certainly true was that since one council house would have been too small for him and his tribe two had to be made into one, and of course rent and rates were paid for by the community. He was accused of using his children as blackmail. People who would not have minded letting him and his wives starve were not prepared to see his children go hungry or homeless. They were convinced that it was deliberate policy on his part always to have two or three under five. Some felt that he ought to be prohibited from having so many, but in a free country how could that be done? Besides, his offspring were all nice children if not particularly bright. Neither their teachers nor the police ever found them troublesome. Fair-minded people too, though they could not say it, thought it, that if there was a war and Britain needed bomb-fodder Billy would have contributed more than his share. Whether it was sly policy, as some maintained, or genuine virtuousness, Billy went to chapel regularly, never stepped inside a public house, never smoked, and never looked at any women except his two wives. If only he had had a good job he would have been an exemplary citizen.

The mishap mentioned, when his canoe overturned, spilling him into the raging stream or rather Barlinnie Prison, was never fully understood, not even by the Sheriff who sentenced him. Was it a navigational blunder or had he intentionally taken a risk? Whatever the reason Billy, at the age of fifty-five when he was on his second wife, who was twenty years younger than himself, his first having died of cancer, took a job without letting the Welfare authorities know. What puzzled the people of Lunderston, and the Sheriff as well, was why so expert a paddler should have taken such a public and conspicuous job, if his intention had been to defraud. He was employed as caretaker of the Queen's Hall, so-called because it had been opened by the Queen some years before. Many functions were held in it, attended by a variety of townspeople, among them no doubt social security officials. Assisted by two of his sons Billy performed his duties well. Everybody knew that the wage he was earning wouldn't be enough to keep him and his family, then numbering thirteen, and would have to be supplemented by Welfare, but no one thought that Billy would be so stupid or rash as not to notify the authorities, so that they could deduct the amount from his Welfare allowances. After three months he was found out, because, it was rumoured, of an anonymous letter. He was arrested, tried, and sentenced to three months in Barlinnie. Anyone in court that sunny August morning would have been more impressed by the prisoner than by the Sheriff. The latter wasn't vindictive but he was sarcastic whereas the former was meek and courteous, merely saying that he was sorry if he had done wrong but his family at the time had needed the money, his wife being pregnant again, and one of his children, wee Bridget, dying of leukaemia.

Most Lunderstonians thought that Billy had got what he deserved, though keeping him in jail was an expensive way of punishing him. Some were affected by his plea from the dock not to be separated from his 'wee yins', and gifts of money were sent in secret to his wife. What ought to be done with

Billy, someone suggested, was that his knowledge of social security rules and regulations should be made use of and he should be given a job as a smeller-out of fraudsters; not in Lunderston of course, where everybody was honest, but in Glasgow, say, where the fly men came from.

Though Billy's knowledge of the rules and regulations was indeed considerable he decided to pass the time in prison improving it. Every free minute was spent in studying the booklets and pamphlets on social security with which the prison library was well supplied. The other prisoners nicknamed him the Professor. They consulted him and were given useful advice. They told him that when he got out he should set up as a consultant. Billy just nodded. The idea had already occurred to him. He knew that millions of pounds went unclaimed by people unaware of their entitlement. He could make it his business to advise them, particularly if they were old. He would do it out of kindness and expect no payment, this in any case would have to be declared and would be ruthlessly deducted.

During his stay in prison wee Bridget died. He was allowed out to attend her funeral.

When he came home his wife Lizzie noticed the difference in him. He had always been quiet because he hadn't anything to say, but now he was quiet because he seemed to be thinking hard all the time. He was as patient as ever with the 'wee yins' but he asked for her co-operation in keeping them out of the small boxroom which, to her mystification, he fitted out as an office. From Jack Murgatroyd, who kept a junk shop, he bought a worm-eaten desk, a tin filing cabinet, and an old typewriter with Ys and Ps missing. Lizzie became alarmed. A credulous watcher of television thrillers, she thought that while in Barlinnie he must have joined a gang of big-time crooks and was helping them to plan a robbery. He assured her that what he was going to do was legal, though the law might not like it. They had sent him to jail because he had claimed more than he was legally entitled to. Nobody was sending to jail those, including the Minister himself, who, knowing that thousands of people were getting less than their due, did nothing about it. That was a swindle too, worse than his.

Lizzie, a simple soul, was afraid of the powerful forces which had taken her husband from her and put him in prison. She could not see how Billy, even if he practised typing every day, could get the better of them. But she was nursing wee Gerry at the time and was more worried by the paucity of milk in her breasts.

Billy's business as a consultant had small beginnings, but then so had Carnegie's. He drew up a list of people he knew who were on Welfare or ought to have been. At the top was Mrs Sneddon, aged seventy-five, a widow, who lived in the same housing scheme as himself. He had seen her once in the supermarket buying one banana. She was always poorly dressed. She had arthritis and her hands were covered with chilblains. He suspected that her house was very cold. She suffered but did not complain.

He was waiting by her gate one icy December morning. As she approached she walked slowly and stiffly. She had no children. His Lizzie, he thought, when she was old and widowed, would never be lonely and would be well looked after. Tears came into his eyes, only partly caused by the bitter wind.

'It's yourself, Mrs Sneddon,' he said.

She didn't want to be seen talking to him. 'Wha did you think it wad be?'

He noticed her covering with a piece of paper the can of cat food in her basket. She would go hungry herself to make sure her cat was fed. But she was afraid that the men who paid her pension might be angry with her for wasting some of it on a cat. It was, he reflected, the most honest and most deserving who were most afraid of the authorities. If he helped her at least her cat would be grateful.

'That's a cauld wind,' he said.

'Whit else wad you expect in December?'

'Is your hoose nice and warm, Mrs Sneddon?'

'That's my business, Billy McShane, and nane o' yours.' Another thing she had against him was that he was a Catholic. She, who never went to church, proudly called herself a Protestant.

'If you'd let me, Mrs Sneddon, I think I could help you.'

'How could you help me? You helped yourself, and we ken whaur it got you. I shouldnae be talking to you. I've always been respectable.'

'It's like this, Mrs Sneddon. The government –.'

'Don't daur say onything to me against the government. I've voted Conservative a' my life. So did my auld man when he was alive.'

Many old poor people like her voted Conservative to prove their respectability. Billy himself never voted. No government, Labour or Tory, could blame him for putting them in.

'The government has decided, Mrs Sneddon, that people in your position should get extra benefits. Blankets, for instance, if you need them.'

'I've got enough blankets.'

'Extra money for coal, or to pay for electricity.'

'I'm no' going on the parish at my age.'

'It wouldn't be like that at all. You wouldn't say the Queen's on the parish, would you?'

'Don't daur miscall the Queen to me, Billy McShane.'

'I wasn't miscalling her. I was just saying that what she gets and is glad to take is her legal entitlement. It's the same with you.'

'I've never grudged the Queen a penny, though, mind you, I'm no sae sure about a' her hanger-ons.'

'Can I come in wi' you for a minute or twa? I'd like to tell you aboot the benefits you're entitled to and how to go aboot getting them.'

'Why should you want to help me?'

'Because, if you'll pardon me for saying it, you need it.'

'It's be the first time I ever had a jilebird in my hoose.'

'I'm sorry if you feel like that, Mrs Sneddon.'

'But you can come in if you like. These benefits, I've sometimes wondered aboot them. Naebody tells me onything.'

Humbly he followed her into the house.

It was icy-cold. He could see no form of heating. There was an electric fire but it was switched off. Her cat as it came to meet her was too chilled to miaow. The first thing she did, before taking off her coat and hat, was open the can and fork it into a dish. It was, Billy noticed, one of the most expensive brands.

'He'll eat nae ither kind,' she said.

Even then she did not remove hat and coat. Billy suspected that she always kept them on.

'The first thing you need,' he said, 'is a heating allowance. I'll see aboot that this very day. Switch on that electric fire. Not just one bar but two. Don't worry. I'll see you get the money to pay the bill.'

As well as a heating allowance he got her an increased rent and rates rebate, a home help, for she was too arthritic to do her own housework, new blankets, for the ones she had were worn and thin, new spectacles and new false teeth. He filled in all the forms for her and took them to the office, where he was regarded with a mixture of suspicion, shame, and resentment. They knew that he was doing for Mrs Sneddon what they should have done for her long ago. He was trying to show them up. It was his way of getting revenge.

'We hope, Mr McShane,' said the manager, grimly facetious,

'that you're not going to do this kind of thing for everybody in Lunderston.'

'Just them that need it,' Billy replied.

Not only Mrs Sneddon's cat was grateful, so was she.

'They say you're a guid-for-nothing rogue, Billy McShane, and I've said it myself, but you've helped me when naebody else bothered, and I'm thankfu'. You're a guid man, in your ain way.'

That was Billy's first success. Others followed.

It became a joke in the town that Billy had set up as a consultant. People asked him when he was putting up his brass plate, like a lawyer. Welfare officials were dumbfounded when applicants, previously turned down, reapplied, with Billy's help, and were successful. 'That's no' whit Billy McShane told us,' they would say, and the clerks, consulting higher authorities, would discover that Billy was right.

There were secret consultations between Welfare officials and the law. What McShane was doing wasn't a crime, at any rate not yet, but it was an impertinent and costly interference. If there was someone like him in every town in the country it would cost the Exchequer millions. If a way could be found to make him mind his own business, without causing a hulla-balloo in the newspapers, then the sooner the better. Did he demand payment for his services? If he did, he could be had for not declaring it as earnings.

Bewildered old women were slyly quizzed. They displeased Sergeant Jackson with their praise of McShane.

'Mr McShane never asked me for as much as a cup o' tea. You and your kind wad hae left me to starve or freeze to daith. It's Mr McShane I hae to thank for being as weel as I am. I should think you'd hae better things to do than speiring aboot a man that likes to help his neebors, like the Bible says.'

The nonplussed sergeant had a word with Billy himself,

at a street corner, making it appear that the meeting was accidental and friendly.

'I hear you're a busy man these days, Billy.'

'You micht say that, sergeant.'

'With a' these fees you get you should be weel-aff.'

'Whit fees?'

'Now, Billy, don't tell me you put yourself to a' that trouble for nothing.'

'I get the thanks of people that needed help. That's not nothing. That's better than money, wouldn't you say?'

'You're talking, Billy, as if the extra money you get for them comes out of your pocket. Whereas it comes out of mine, for, you see, I pay taxes.'

'Then you're luckier than them that don't, for it means you've gota weel-paid job.'

'They tell me you attend chapel regularly.'

'Every Sunday.'

'In his sermons doesn't Father Murphy say anything about minding your own business and keeping out of trouble?'

'He says in a' his sermons that helping ithers should be oor main business in life.'

The sergeant had heard that when people distressed by lack of money came to Father Murphy he sent them to Billy.

'Just a word in your ear, Billy. We're keeping an eye on you.'

As the sergeant prepared to walk away Billy said, humorously, 'Whit if I had a wee tape-recorder in my waistcoat pocket, sergeant? Whit if I sent it to the *Sunday Mail*?'

The sergeant smiled. He could be seen to be thinking carefully before he spoke again. Having a tape-recorder in his pocket was just the thing this sleekit villian would do. 'Where would you get the money to buy a tape-recorder, Billy?'

'Maybe from Welfare, if I proved to them I needed it for my protection.'

'Don't joke with me.'

'It was you that sought this conversation, sergeant.'

'I just wanted to warn you, in a friendly manner, to keep out of trouble. You've been inside once, Billy. Wasn't that enough?'

'Is that a threat, sergeant?'

The sergeant realised he was in a position where anything he said would sound like a threat. 'Like yourself, Billy, I'm in the business of advising folk, not threatening them.' But even that, listened to in a newspaper office, would sound sinister.

As he stalked off, with the dignity his uniform called for, the sergeant could not resist glancing back. It had struck him that McShane had been a bad colour, with a bluish tinge to his lips. Perhaps it was true that he had a heart condition. There he was now, walking like a man of eighty, yet he couldn't be much older than sixty. With luck he could soon be summoned before a Judge that he wouldn't be able to take in, with his hypocrisy about helping others. Not a Catholic himself, the sergeant none the less approved of their belief in posthumous punishments. A little roasting would do Billy's soul a lot of good. His youngest child was now fourteen, so there would be no 'wee yins' to miss him. Nobody would, except scroungers, workshys, layabouts, and scrimshankers.

But the sergeant was wrong, as he was to see for himself. A few weeks after his conversation with Billy the latter was found dead in his bed. His procreative endeavours had done for him at last, jested the town's wits. He was only sixty-two. The funeral was private. There were jokes about its opulence. Even in his coffin, the best in the undertaker's stock, Billy was seeing to it that he was buried in style, no doubt at the State's expense. There were three black Rolls Royces for his family. But what most disgusted and perplexed the sergeant at the cemetery gates, a duty he had given himself, was the mass of people, many of them elderly, who had come not to jeer but to mourn. Old men shook their heads sadly, old women dabbed their eyes with their hankies. There were cries of 'Goodbye, Billy' and 'God bless you, Billy.'

Well, Billy, thought the sergeant, as the hearse and the limousines passed through the gates, it's a pity you haven't got a tape-recorder hidden in your waistcoat pocket today.

'He did a lot mair guid than harm,' said one old man to another.

Men buried in Westminster Abbey would have been proud of such an epitaph, thought the sergeant. Yet, Billy, to be truthful, putting aside the sentimentalities of death, what were you all your life but a parasite that never worked nor wanted?

The Cabinet Minister and
the Garbage Collector

THE SCOTS HAVE ALWAYS been a more democratic nation than the English. Whether this was because they have always been too poor to afford hierarchies, as the English jeer, or because as the Scots themselves point out every Scotsman is born with the belief that we are 'a' Jock Tamson's bairns', a phrase untranslatable into English, the fact remains that as long ago as 1603 James Vl of Scotland, disgruntled at being spoken to as if he was an errant human being like everyone else, scurried off to England where he knew that those lovers of rank would take seriously his nonsensical claim to be divine and therefore infallible. Many of the Scots so-called nobility, sycophants to a man, fled south with him. A hundred and four years later what remained of the Scots aristocracy sold their country to the English, despite the common people's protests. Whatever influence they might have had on the life of the nation was forfeited forever. They were, indeed, glad to relinquish it. Henceforth they spent most of their time in England, sending their sons to English schools to acquire pukka English accents. In Scotland they were not missed.

Take a typical small Scottish town like Lunderston. There is no lord or lady of the manor to whom everybody instinctively kowtows. The family who once owned all the land round about still own the Big House, but they mean nothing to the town and are seldom seen in it. If they do appear in a shop they are treated like any other customers. Perhaps their accent is humorously referred to, because the upperclass English style of speaking is always an amusement to Scots, who, quite unfairly of course, cannot bring themselves to believe that that lah-di-dah palaver could possibly be used to discuss such real and pertinent matters as rising prices or sick children or deaths from cancer. If in spite of that handicap aristocratic families in Scotland try to be pleasant and friendly to those they consider their inferiors credit is given them, for it is appreciated how much more difficult it must be for them, in their isolated mansions screened by trees, to be human and companionable, than it is for ordinary folk who live close together in streets, roads, avenues, crescents, vennels, and alleys.

Who then are the people in Lunderston who matter most? Who are they who, because of their superior culture and wealth, are looked up to and shown instinctive deference by the rest? They do not exist, though there are a few who like to think of themselves as the elite. The people who live in the villas along the sea-front or in the bigger houses up in Alisa Park are obviously better-off and better-educated than those who live in tenements or council housing-schemes, but they are never thought of as superior, only as luckier. In an election for the council a man or woman from a housing-scheme is as likely to be elected as one from a villa. It used to be the case that the Captain of the Golf Club was chosen because of his professional standing in the town, being a lawyer or doctor or accountant, but nowadays it is hardworking service as a committee member that counts, and no one is surprised or offended if a joiner or a publican is given the honour.

What most of all has helped the Scots to remain democratic, in the many small towns from Thurso in the north to Kelso in the south, is the existence of truly comprehensive schools, which take in children from villas and tenements alike. These institutions, proudly called Academies or Grammar Schools or High Schools, are in some cases hundreds of years old. They are the reason why in Scotland lawyers and labourers speak with the same accent, though the latter might use more old-fashioned Scotticisms. Since every child of secondary age attends them it follows that there are among their pupils some who will go on to University and others who will pass no examinations and win no certificates. It would be an exaggeration to say that the bright and the dim associate freely, for they are usually in different classes, but it sometimes does happen that boys, or girls, who were friends in primary school continue the friendship in the secondary school, though one will study Latin and French while the other is asked to concentrate on woodwork and gardening. An example of these improbable friendships was that between Neil McLeod and Archie Abercrombie of Lunderston.

They first met when they went to Lunderston Primary School at the age of five, though their homes, one a council flat and the other a semi-detached villa, were not far from each other. Both were only children. Even at primary school Neil was brilliant, while Archie was, frankly, a dunce. Yet it was Neil's parents who lived in the flat and Archie's in the villa. Mr McLeod was a council roadman and Mr Abercrombie a lawyer's clerk. The Abercrombies were very ambitious for their son, hoping that he would be a lawyer one day. The McLeods on the contrary were uneasy at their son's successes, they wanted him to get a good steady council job like his father when he left school. It would have been difficult to say who were the more upset, the McLeods or the Abercrombies, when the former were assured by the Careers Officer that their son Neil was very clever and must be given his chance at University, and the latter were told tactfully that their Archie, though one of the happiest lads in the school, was academically unsuited. It was as well, hinted the Careers Officer, unconsciously sprinkling salt on the wound, that Archie was so cheerfully unambitious. Asked to write on a form what career he would like to pursue after leaving school he had written 'Garbidge Colector'. He had not been having a joke at his own or the school's expense; he had meant it. Challenged, he had said that it was a very useful job and meant being out in the open air.

Though the boys were such close friends and were often in each other's house their parents seldom met. The McLeods were pleased and flattered that their son had a friend who lived in a villa. Secretly they wished that their Neil was more like Archie, with whom they got on very well, for he liked the same kind of TV programmes that they did and talked about the same kind of things, whereas their Neil professed contempt for soap operas like Dallas and had no time for local gossip. As for Archie's parents, they were fascinated by young Neil, who even at fourteen read the *Guardian*, was knowledgeable about politics, world affairs, science, and literature, and was ambitious to become a lawyer. It was a consolation to them, but not much, that their Archie was a big strong fair-haired boy with excellent eyesight, whereas Neil was small, fat, and myopic, needing thick-lensed glasses.

One wet afternoon Mrs Abercrombie eavesdropped on a conversation between the two boys. They were assembling a model aeroplane. She had noticed, with anguished pride, that Archie was more skilful at this simple task than his brainier friend.

It was shortly before the summer holidays. Archie had found himself a job helping Mr Stewart, the boat-hirer. He had the strength to pull boats up over the shingle. He wouldn't mind, he remarked, as he neatly glued on a wing, working with boats all his life. His mother could have wept at his lack of ambition, especially as she had then to listen to Neil saying, with his usual precocious assurance, that he was going to be a Member of Parliament.

'I thought you were going to be a lawyer,' said Archie.

'So I am. Lots of MPs are lawyers.'

'That's not fair. It would mean you having two jobs when lots of people can't get one. Anyway, what good are Members of Parliament?'

'The country has to be governed, Archie.'

'Can't people look after themselves?'

'The rich can, the poor can't.'

Mrs Abercrombie had heard that young Neil was already a member of Lunderston Labour Party. She and her husband, both good Conservatives, had debated whether or not to discourage Archie from associating with him, for they believed everything the *Daily Express* told them about socialists.

'Is that why you want to be a Member of Parliament?' asked Archie. 'So that you can be rich.'

'No. It's because I think that the wealth of the country should be more fairly distributed.'

Go on, Archie, cried Mrs Abercrombie inwardly, tell the wee humbug that Labour politicians are in it for the money too. Tell him that they end up in the House of Lords.

But Archie would never have attributed discreditable motives to his friend. 'Politics is just talk,' he said. 'On the television they're talking a' the time. Whit good's that? I like daeing things wi' my hands.'

Don't say 'whit' and 'a'' and 'daeing' and 'wi'', was Mrs Abercrombie's cry now. Say 'what' and 'all' and 'doing' and 'with'.

The wee know-all was speaking. 'Thomas Carlyle, a famous Scottish writer, said that there were two kinds of men he honoured, the kind that earned his living with his hands and the kind that earned it with his brains.'

'Did he say who should get paid most?'

'I don't think he mentioned that.'

'Does a teacher earn his living with his brains?'

'Yes, I would say so.'

'Except when he's giving somebody the strap. Do teachers get paid more than garbage collectors?'

'I think so, Archie, though they're always grumbling about not getting paid enough.'

'A garbage collector's job's mair important. He keeps away the plague. Teachers just tell you things you don't want to know.'

'Good teachers are supposed to make their subjects interesting.'

'I think one day garbage collectors will get paid more than teachers.'

'I doubt it, Archie. It's a matter of qualifications. You don't have to go to college to be a garbage collector.'

'One day there will be nae schools. Everybody will get educated by watching television.'

'It's possible, Archie. Who knows what electronic wonders are in store for us?'

When he was twenty-four Archie, through the influence of a Tory councillor, achieved his ambition and got a permanent job as a garbage collector. He was one of those who leapt off the lorry, grabbed the black bags, tossed them in, and leapt on again. Sometimes they burst and Archie showed his pride in his work by clearing up the mess with his bare hands, unlike his colleagues, who left the used tea-bags, the empty cartons, the greasy remnants of food, and all the other miscellaneous rubbish on the pavement. He hoped to be promoted to driver one day, for he had acquired a driving licence. His parents grieved that he had not done better for himself, but they were also relieved that, after a number of temporary jobs since leaving school, he had at last found one that would keep him in Lunderston and bring him a pension. Moreover, with overtime, he was able to earn more than many teachers. It broke their hearts though when he came home in the evenings, tired, with his boots and hands stinking, and whistling cheerfully. It was his cheerfulness that they found heart-rending.

It was not likely, they warned each other, that he would meet and marry a refined educated girl, for such girls preferred to marry schoolteachers. Therefore they were not surprised, though horrified, when he brought home Tessa McPhie and blithely announced that they were going to get married. Tessa was pregnant and didn't want an abortion, she wanted 'Erchie's wean.' About the only thing his parents could find in her favour was that she wasn't a Catholic, though her family couldn't have been more numerous and scruffy if they had been. Mrs McPhie was of tinker stock, which was probably worse. In Lunderston, where equality prevailed, you were not permitted to look down on people as your inferiors; you were expected to avoid them, as you would dogs' dirt. That was how Mrs Abercrombie would have liked to treat the McPhies, but unfortunately she couldn't, since her darling son, her only child, was determined to marry one of them. The girl herself was a tall buxom red-haired hussy of twenty, given to coarse language. For example, when explaining how she had got pregnant, she had blamed Erchie's 'fucking carelessness' in forgetting to bring a French letter. Though she said it jocosely, and indeed affectionately, it pained Mr and Mrs Abercrombie to hear. They tried hard to dissuade Archie, his mother with tears, his father with shouts of anger, but to no avail. Archie said he loved Tessa, and even if he didn't he would marry her because of the wean. What if it isn't yours, cried his mother, who had heard that Tessa had several lovers. That wouldn't matter, replied Archie, so long as it was Tessa's. Though simple, he could be stubborn, and the marriage took place, a riotous affair at which some of Tessa's relatives got drunk. Thanks again to the machinations of the Tory councillor the newly-weds were given a council flat, in the same tenement where the McLeods had lived. *They* had since moved to a bungalow bought for them by Neil, now a lawyer in Edinburgh.

Neil was also a rising star in the Labour Party and would be a candidate at the next General Election. He had already been seen and heard on Scottish television, speaking with the same canny good sense as in school debates, except that now he did it more pompously or more weightily, according to the political sympathies of those who heard him. He was still short, stout, and bespectacled, and was showing signs of premature baldness. He was engaged to the daughter of an Edinburgh lawyer, she too was a lawyer. 'Heaven knows how she gets on with his parents,' said Mrs Abercrombie, 'for they're not just common, they're also ignorant and have never anything to say for themselves. I don't suppose she'll visit them often.'

When Tessa and Archie's child was born, Tessa wheeled it to her mother-in-law's every day. Mrs Abercrombie tried at first to treat it with indifference, but how could she, when it was a boy, with the same blue eyes, fair hair, and happy chuckle of its father?

Mrs Abercrombie and Mrs McLeod met one day in the supermarket. The latter was shy, the former forward, though it should have been the other way about.

'I see Neil's fairly making a name for himself,' said Mrs Abercrombie.

Mrs McLeod just smiled.

'He's not married yet, is he?'

'No. Sheila doesnae believe in getting married too young.'

'Too young? What age is she, then?'

'Twenty-four, like Neil himself. And like your Archie.'

'I wouldn't call that very young. But maybe they're waiting till they've got enough money to buy a grand big house.'

'I don't think it's that. Sheila's nae snob, you ken.'

'Maybe she's not fond of children?'

'She's never said.'

'Well, I'm glad Archie's wife is. They'll have more than one, I'm glad to say.'

'He's a very bonny wee boy, Mrs Abercrombie, very like Archie.'

'We think so too.'

'Tessa McPhie's a nice sensible lassie, though maybe a wee bit rough in her ways. She'll keep Archie right.'

'I don't think he needs his wife to do that for him, Mrs McLeod. By the way, Neil seems to have little time for his old friends these days. I mean, when was he last in Lunderston?'

'He's very busy. But he was here aboot three weeks ago.'

'Archie never mentioned it.'

'He didn't have time to visit Archie. He was very sorry aboot it. You ken whit guid freen's they still are.'

'Well, I'm sure Archie has plenty of friends here in Lunderston.'

'So he has. He's always been well-liked, your Archie.'

And your Neil has always been a conceited puke. But Mrs Abercrombie didn't say it.

'And his job wi' the garbage lorry makes him so weel-kent.'

Was that a dig? wondered Mrs Abercrombie. A glance at the timid anxious face reassured her. Mrs McLeod had not been sneering at Archie's job. Perhaps in her heart she wished that her Neil was a garbage collector too, living in Lunderston and married to a Lunderston girl.

'Well, give Neil my regards, Mrs McLeod, next time you see him.'

'I'll do that, Mrs Abercrombie. He often talks aboot the good times he and Archie had in your hoose.'

By the time he was forty-five Neil McLeod was MP for a Lothian constituency and a Cabinet Minister in a Labour government. Political pundits were tipping him as a future Prime Minister. As required he had shed whatever revolutionary zeal he had had in his youth and now made circumspect speeches that won the respect of his Tory opponents and enraged the left-wing members of his Party. He was now an advocate, with the letters QC after his name. His polemical skill and imperturbable manner made it difficult for political friends and foes alike to know exactly where he stood on many matters. It was of course the proper stance for an MP aiming at the top. As for his parents, they were so much in awe of him that everything he did or said was mystical and wonderful. They found indeed that their daughter-in-law Sheila, though she had been educated at private schools, was easier to talk to than Neil, for, unlike him, she liked a good blether about ordinary things and made sure that her two children, Ian at Edinburgh Academy, and Marjorie at an exclusive girls' school, were respectful to their plebeian grandparents.

Neil travelled a great deal on government business and never failed to send Archie postcards, addressed in his own hand-writing. These, from places like Brussels, Geneva, Washington, and Tokyo were kept in a cabinet in Archie's living-room and shown to all visitors. As someone said they could be worth money one day.

Archie at forty-five was still leaping off and on the lorry. His parents were indignant that he had not been given promotion, but he himself made light of it, saying that he was more suited to a job that needed physical strength. As the father of five he also needed patience and good humour. His oldest, Archie Junior, was twenty-one and a student at college, having inherited his mother's quickness of mind; Mary his youngest was three; and there were three in between. This prolificity had caused his mother to wonder if the McPhies were secret Catholics. Once, when Tessa was pregnant for the fifth time, her mother-in-law had boldly remarked that surely four would have been enough. Tessa had laughed. 'That's so, Mrs Abercrombie, but, you see, that eedjit of a son of yours learned long ago that the easiest kind of contraception was for me to be pregnant. It's damn near every night wi' him, you ken, bless his big cock.' For Tessa, though a matron with three daughters, still used outrageous language. Once Neil had taken Sheila to visit Archie and Tessa. According to Archie Tessa and Sheila had got on well, but his mother didn't believe him: he was so hopelessly good-natured himself that he never noticed when people, smiling on the surface, were scowling beneath.

Every year on the last Saturday in August Lunderston held what it called its Highland Games, the name being justified because tossing-the-caber was included and the mountains of Arran could be seen from the stadium. A prominent personage was invited to open them, usually someone with a title. When it was announced in the Gazette that the Rt Honourable Neil McLeod, PC, MP, QC, MA, was to open them that particular year there were some grumbles from Tories, but most people thought that he deserved the honour, for what it was worth. He had been born and bred in the town. His parents still lived there. He had kissed the Queen's hand. No man could be more eligible.

So there he was, that sunny August afternoon, on the dais in front of the stand, wearing a suit that must have cost a hundred pounds and looking not a bit overwhelmed. Speaking into a microphone he was heard all over the field and even in the beer tent behind the stand, where it so happened Archie Abercrombie and two friends were chatting. Like everybody else, even the pipers tuning up, they were quiet as they listened to the important man from London, who had been born in Lunderston and still spoke with a Lunderstonian accent, rather a prim version it was true but authentic enough. He did very well. He knew what to say, no more and no less, and he said it sensibly, unlike the man who'd done it last year, Sir Something-or-other, who had had too much to drink at lunch and havered for fifteen minutes about Scotland's glorious past, when he ought to have known that five were long enough or even, considering his theme, three.

'Neil's a pal o' mine,' said Archie, modestly. 'He's coming to see Tessa and me after the games.'

They had heard about his friendship with the Cabinet Minister and were impressed, though a little sceptical too. Archie's hands as they gripped a beer can were big, brown, and strong. They had seen McLeod's white flabby hands when he had arrived in the official limousine. They could not believe that men with hands so dissimilar could really be friends, but they did not say so, out of politeness and consideration for Archie whom they liked, all the more because he was a bit simple, and they willingly joined him in a toast to McLeod. Any reason for staying longer in the beer tent before joining their wives was acceptable.

As the Chieftain of the Games, McLeod had to wait until the end. He could not, like many others, sneak off when he became bored. He had to stand on the dais again while the pipers, more than five hundred of them, marched past, playing 'Lunderston Bay', a tune composed for the occasion. Those spectators still remaining admired the way he didn't put his fingers at his brow in a pseudo-salute or his hand on his heart like a daft American, but as a good Scotsman wearing trousers should stood with his arms at his sides. They noticed too that he was still smiling, but then in Parliament he must have listened to hours of speeches even more tedious than the same pipe tune repeated a hundred or so times. They were not to know that his back ached, his ears were numb, and his stomach rumbled with emptiness. What he wanted was to get out of Lunderston as quickly as possible. He and Sheila were to spend the night at Killin Castle, a five-star country house hotel. He had told her they deserved such a treat.

At last it was all over. Sheila and he were driven to where their own car was parked outside the Council Chambers.

'Thank God that's over,' he muttered. He wondered how many votes he had won for the Labour candidate in Lunderston. Not many, he supposed, gloomily. The town was a Tory stronghold.

'I hope you're remembering we promised to drop in on Archie and Tessa.'

'Oh hell!'

'I thought you liked Archie.'

'So I do, but I'm dead tired.'

'So am I. As Tessa would say, my arse is paralysed with sitting on that hard seat for three hours.'

'You know, Sheila, I don't think I could stand Tessa tonight.'

'I thought you found her candour refreshing.'

'I do, usually, but not tonight. Christ, those ducks on the wall.'

'Geese, I think.'

'And those purple plush armchairs. And the smell of chips.'

'You sound like a snob. Don't you remember? "We twa hae rin aboot the braes, and pu'd the gowans fine."'

Neil groaned. Years ago, shortly after the New Year, in Archie's house, after a few drams, he had recited all the verses of Auld Lang Syne. His present groan expressed complicated feelings; embarrassment at the sentimentality, but also shame at that embarrassment. He had often envied Archie his simple view of things; he did so now.

'Apart from your parents, Neil, he's your only connection with your native town. Haven't I heard you say often how dangerous it is for a politician to lose touch with his "ain folk."'

'You're talking as if you enjoyed visiting them.'

'I do. Tessa's great fun, and Archie, without meaning to and without knowing he's doing it, delivers some home truths, which do you good.'

'In what way do they do me good?'

'They disconcert you, and I like that. It reassures me. I know then I married a human being, not a politician.'

'Very funny. All right. But we'll not stay long.'

'Don't worry. They won't press us to stay long. They like to see us, but they know we're not their own kind. I never was, I suppose, so they're comfortable with me. But they're never really at ease with you, Neil. They regard you as if you'd been to outer space and back. They know it's you and yet they're not sure. What have those weird creatures in outer space done to you? You can see them asking themselves that.'

In their yellow Cavalier they drove through the town to Archie's tenement. The streets were thronged. It was a pleasant warm evening. There was a festival atmosphere. All the pubs were busy, with boozers and pipers. As soon as dark fell there would be a fireworks display at the old pier. Some, not all of them men, would be too drunk by then to appreciate it.

'Archie's beginning to drink too much,' said Sheila. 'I was talking to him for a minute at the stadium. There was a stink of beer off his breath.'

'He's always been fond of his pint.'

'It's more than a pint nowadays. Is it possible that even Archie has become disillusioned?'

'What do you mean?'

'He's always been the soul of hopefulness. He's never grumbled. He's been content. He's made other people feel content too. He took a pint for friendship's sake. A cup of kindness. Now it's different.'

'You're imagining things. Tessa would never let him drink to excess.'

'Maybe she's disillusioned too.'

'I don't think she ever had any illusions.'

'Do you remember how she used to tease you? "When are they making you a lord, Neil?"'

'She's never been the brightest of ladies.'

'Is that so? Well, here's a bright lady asking: Will they make you a lord, Neil? Will you let them?'

'Your mother would like it.'

'Whereas yours would be terribly embarrassed. Your mother and Archie, the salt of the earth.'

'But you think in Archie's case it has lost its savour?'

'If it has we're the sufferers, as your mother would say.'

There was no parking space near Archie's tenement so they had to leave the car in a quiet avenue about a quarter of a mile away and walk.

This was the district where Neil had been born and brought up. There had been changes; an open space where Archie and he had played football was now occupied by some small bungalows, and a church was now used as a bingo hall. Still, it was recognisable, and he was pleased when an old woman passing said 'It's yourself, Neil', as if he had never been away. He was even more pleased that he was able to reply 'Hello, Mrs Armstrong.' She did not stop and talk to famous man. She was in too big a hurry to get home. Perhaps she would say to old Bert, if he was still alive, for she herself was well over seventy 'Guess who I saw in the street? Neil McLeod.' Or perhaps she would have forgotten him by the time she got home. She would have more important things to think about.

He smiled.

'It's good for you to be here,' said Sheila.

'Yes.'

Archie's parents had both died and left him their semi detached villa. He had decided, or rather Tessa had decided for him, that he did not want to live among the toffs, so he had sold it and remained in his council tenement, though with the increases in his family he had had to exchange his one-bedroomed flat for one with three bedrooms. Even then it was a tight squeeze. His close was clean enough, though not pipeclayed as in Neil's childhood. Women nowadays were not willing to go down on their knees on hard cement, as Neil's mother had done. There was some graffiti on the walls, neither witty nor obscene.

Outside the Abercrombie's door was a mat, with the word WELCOME worked into it in red, white, and blue letters. The nameplate of brass was inscribed in Gothic script.

It was Tessa who came to the door, with a cigarette in her mouth. She was wearing a tight green jersey and tight green slacks. She was stouter than twenty years ago but was tall and strong enough to carry the burdens of heavy breasts and big behind without stoop or waddle. Her belly though was gross. Was she pregnant again? She was only forty-two, so it was possible, and she looked as lusty as ever, so it was likely.

'Well, look who's here!' she cried. 'I owe Archie a quid. I bet him that amount that you wouldn't come. But I'm glad I lost.' She did not shake hands, but kissed Sheila on the cheek and gave Neil a hug that had him gasping.

In the living-room were Archie, in one of the armchairs, an old shrunken wife whom Neil recognised as Tessa's mother, descended from tinkers, Tessa's sister Bella, fat and moon-faced, and Alfred, Bella's man, who was evidently the drunkest of the four, but good-natured with it. They were all drinking whisky and lemonade. The bottles were on the table, which was set for the evening meal. There was a smell of chips.

Places were made for Sheila and Neil on the sofa, beside Granny McPhie. They were offered drinks and politely declined.

'Can't stay long, I'm afraid,' said Neil 'Got to catch the night sleeper to London.'

'Dae MPs work on Sundays?' asked Bella, shaking her head. She didn't believe MPs ever did any honest work, unlike her Alf who collected scrap iron.

'Often we have to, Bella.'

'Nae fucking wonder then that the country's in a hell of a mess.'

Her mother rebuked her. 'We don't want that kind of language in front of visitors.' She grabbed Sheila's skirt. 'Whit tartan's this then? It's no' the McLeod.'

'No, it's the McKenzie. My maiden name's McKenzie.'

'Why's your man no' wearing a kilt? They were a' saying that as the Chieftain o' the Games he should hae been wearing a kilt. Wi' a name like McLeod he's entitled to wear a kilt.'

'My grandfather lived in the Hebrides all his life,' said Neil, 'and he never once wore a kilt. He never found it a suitable garb for digging peats or rowing a boat.'

'But he was never Chieftain of the Games.'

'Archie was saying you did very well, Neil,' said Tessa.

'Weren't you there yourself, Tessa?'

'Hell no, I stopped going years ago. Mind you, I always liked watching the big fellows tossing their cabers.' She laughed and patted her belly. 'As you can see, Archie's been tossing his.'

Her mother was scandalised. 'Whit kind of talk is that, Tessa McPhie? In front o' visitors too.'

'They're no' juist visitors, mither. They're freen's.'

Sheila seemed not to be offended. 'Will this be your sixth, Tessa?'

'I never had ony,' said Bella, and she began to whimper. 'And we've gi'en up trying. This yin – ' she glared at Alf 'couldnae toss a caber to save his life.'

'We were juist aboot to hae oor tea,' said Tessa. 'Pie and chips. Would you care to join us?'

'No thanks, Tessa,' said Neil, a little too hastily.

'Are you sure, Neil? Baxter's pies? The best in the West of Scotland.'

'Is he still in business?'

'They come from miles to buy his pies. Isn't that so, Archie?'

She felt it was time her husband put in a word. After all, it was his boyhood chum who had called. Archie was smiling but saying nothing. Suddenly he said, 'They were saying at the Games, Neil, that that suit you've got on must hae cost over a hundred pounds.'

'Now, Archie,' said Tessa, 'it's nane of oor business how much Neil's suit cost.'

'Do you mind, Neil, when you had to staun' against the wa' because there was a big patch on your backside?'

'Were you ever as poor as that, Neil?' asked Tessa, laughing.

'Was he ever as shy as that?' asked Sheila.

'He was shy up to the age of eight,' said Archie. 'After that he wasnae shy.'

'I've heard Archie say, Neil,' said Tessa, 'that you were already making speeches when you were eight.'

'Was it the patch on your arse made you a socialist?' asked Bella.

'It may have helped, Bella, but to tell the truth I don't remember it.'

'Archie remembers everything that happened to him when he was a boy,' said Tessa.

Neil, though not quite comfortable, was wishing that his detractors, many of them in his own Party, could have been there to see how much he was at home in the house of a garbage collector. As for Tories, the majority of whom had been educated at public schools, this was the kind of experience forever denied to them, and surely it was what every politician needed if, that was to say, he was in politics not to benefit himself, as cynics sneered, but to promote social justice.

With A Tinge of Yellow

1

THE POSTMAN USUALLY CAME about quarter past eight, just before Marian and he set off for the shop and the two boys for school. That morning, probably because of the rain, he was twenty minutes late. They met him in the street.

'Awfu' morning, Mr Nairn,' he said, delving into his bag.

'It is that,' replied Robert.

Seldom interested in the mail, Bob and Alistair cycled off in their yellow capes.

Under her red umbrella their mother waved goodbye, calling to them to be careful.

There were three letters. One was from America. The handwriting was so familiar that tears came into his eyes.

He could not help blurting out, 'It's from Cathie.'

He was afraid to look at Marian. She wouldn't be looking angry or hurt. She would be trying to pretend, and doing it dreadfully well, that nothing had happened, that he had no letter from America in his hand, for the girl who had sent it, their daughter Cathie, twenty years old, did not exist.

He had thought that only in books and films did a mother, especially one who went to church and was liked by her neighbours, ever say of her only daughter 'She pleased herself. So I'll please myself. I don't want to hear her name spoken in this house again. If anyone does I'll walk out, so help me.'

But Marian had said it and afterwards had shown that she meant it.

The terrible thing was that a good part of him, no a big part of him, for there was nothing good about it, agreed with her. What Cathie had done was unforgivable.

There at the gate, with the rain dripping from his nose, he felt like a deadly pain his lifelong inadequacy. If he was to be faithful to Marian and keep the promise he had given her, whether or not unwisely, he must tear up Cathie's letter without reading it and drop the pieces in the gutter among the dead leaves. But he could not. He loved Cathie, he would love her all his life. This letter might be an appeal for help. If he ignored it he would despise himself even more than he did now. If he heeded it he would run the risk of losing his wife.

He crumpled up the letter as if it didn't matter and shoved it into his raincoat pocket. He tried to give the impression that he would get rid of it as soon as he found a trash can.

Their shop, a licensed grocer's, was only two hundred yards along the street. On their way to it they passed Mrs Dalgleish, a former customer. 'Nothing personal about it, Mr Nairn, and I'm very sorry, but you charge 102p for a packet of cornflakes, which is 7p more than I have to pay in the supermarket.' He had tried to explain that he had high overheads and gave a personal service, but it had been useless. There were others like her. Nowadays money was everything.

That morning she passed them with a civil grumble about the weather, but Robert knew what she was thinking. 'That's the Nairns. Their shop's failing. But that's not the worst of it. About a year ago their daughter, the joy of their hearts, married an American sailor. Of course lots of girls from the West of Scotland have married American sailors since the base on the Holy Loch was opened up. But Cathie Nairn married a *black* American sailor. God knows why. She had plenty of her own kind to choose from. A good-looking girl, with fair hair. Her poor parents never got a chance to stop it. Cathie and her black went off to America. The shame of it nearly killed her mother, and no wonder. Her father? Well, Robert Nairn's not much of a man really, nobody would ever call him bright, and he's always been under his wife's thumb. She made him disown Cathie. I heard she made him swear it on the Bible. What kind of a girl was Cathie? Well that's the funny thing. A nice girl, shy, timid even. The black must have taken advantage of her. They say he was an officer. But you can be sure that wherever she is – in California I believe – she's discovering what a fearful mistake she's made.'

That was what the whole town was still thinking.

Business was slack that morning. There were many opportunities for him and Marian to talk about the letter. None was taken. He could have read it himself in the small WC but shame prevented him.

At half-past twelve Marian left to prepare their lunch at home. The boys ate at school.

She had not asked him if he had destroyed the letter; that would have been acknowledging its existence. For the same reason she had not forbidden him to read it. But if he did and she found out she would hate him.

He had noticed in himself too a terrifying deterioration. He had always been a bit weak, too ready to take the easy way out; but he had always thought himself as decent as most men. Now in this trap in which he was caught he sometimes felt vicious impulses. He thought of running away and abandoning them all. It crossed his mind to burn down the shop and claim the insurance money. He lusted after pink-cheeked, big-busted Mrs Hunter who came into the shop every morning for milk and rolls.

Another customer now came in, just as he was about to close for lunch, old Mrs Strachan, wanting two ounces of cheese, a can of cat food, and a yesterday's loaf that cost 2p less than today's. She was very poor, but she was one of the few who had pleaded with him and Marian not to be too hard on Cathie. Ever since he had given her generous measure.

When she was gone he took out the letter, feeling guilty like a thief. He saw with anguish how short it was. 'Dear Mum and Dad, I know I shouldn't be writing this for you don't want to hear from me, but I thought you might like to know that I'm going to have a baby in about three weeks. I'm afraid. I'd like very much if one of you could be here.'

It had been bound to happen. His lovely fair-skinned yellow-haired daughter must have done with the black many times the act that could produce a child.

He groaned and beat his head with his fist.

After he had shut the shop he did not go straight home. He had to do some thinking before he faced Marian.

Whatever its colour the child would be his grandchild. It was his natural duty to defend its right to exist and be given the same chance to prosper as any other child. The more it was despised and rejected the more staunchly must he defend it. And there was Cathie herself, afraid and asking for help.

He telephoned a travel agent in Greenock, where he wasn't known, and asked how much it would cost to fly to San Diego and back.

'It would depend on when you want to go, Mr Nairn. If you can give forty-five days' notice you'll get it a good deal cheaper.'

'I can't wait that long.'

'It would mean ordinary economy fare in that case, £550 return. From Heathrow.'

'Thanks. I'll let you know.'

All in it would cost at least £700, for there would be hotel expenses. He didn't have that much in the bank or anything like it.

2

When he and Marian were alone they ate in the kitchen, where it was cosy. There was always a fresh cloth on the table. Everything was clean. Thus Marian proved herself a good wife. Today in her pink and white overall she looked bonny as well as homely. She had the same fair hair as Cathie.

Seated at the table, waiting for his soup to be ladled out, he said, with his eyes shut. 'Sorry, Marian, but we've just got to talk about that letter from Cathie. I've read it.'

Carefully, without spilling any, she returned the pot of soup to the stove. She did not look at him or speak as she walked out. He heard her going slowly up the stairs.

He hated her for putting his love for Cathie and his courage as a father to too severe a test.

She should at least have discussed it. She had no right to treat him like a leper.

It was a kind of leprosy they all had. It wasn't their fingers and toes that were being eaten away, it was their dependence on one another. Even the boys had become less communicative.

He must not give in too quickly this time.

With the letter in his hand he went upstairs.

The bedroom door was locked. Inside Marian seemed to be weeping. He wondered if it was a sign of remorse or at least of regret.

'Listen, Marian,' he said. 'She's going to have a baby. That's unbearable. I agree it's unbearable. But she's afraid, and God knows she's only twenty. She wants one of us to be with her. She'd prefer you, Marian, you're her mother, but if you don't feel up to it then I'll go, though God knows I don't want to either.'

She had stopped weeping. Perhaps the change of heart, the flowering of pity, which he had been praying for for months, was at last taking place.

'But I need your agreement,' he went on. 'We'd have to raise the money somehow. It would cost at least £700, just for one, so it's out of the question both of us going. I'm willing to do what you've been at me for years to do. I'll sell the shop and go back to my old trade. And you can go back to your old job in Sinclair's.'

He had been a baker, and a good one. Anyone of the three bakery firms in the town would be glad to have him. For years Marian had worked for Sinclair the chemist in his dispensing room. He was always asking her to come back. She had been competent and conscientious.

She didn't answer. She seemed to be moving about.

'We can't turn our backs on her for the rest of our lives,' he said.

The door opened. She had a suitcase in her hand. Her face was pale and twisted, her eyes hard and red.

'I've just got one thing to ask,' she said, harshly.

'What is it, Marian? I'm anxious to be reasonable.'

'Are you serious?'

'About selling the shop? Yes, I am.'

'About going to America.'

'Yes, but I'd like to discuss it with you.'

She pushed past him. At the foot of the stairs she put on her raincoat.

'Where are you going?' he shouted down.

But he knew. Her crony Margaret Seaton would take her in and pour more poison into her ear.

He lost his nerve. 'If you go to that bitch Seaton don't bother to come back.'

As she went out she closed the door firmly.

'What about the boys?' he howled.

But she was gone, out of hearing.

'I don't give a fuck,' he muttered, weeping. 'I'll go if I want to. I don't need your blessing.'

3

Ten days later he arrived in San Diego shortly after eight at night. He felt tired, disoriented, and self-piteous.

The taxi that picked him up outside the airport building had a black driver. It seemed a bad omen.

'I'm a stranger here,' he said, politely, almost meekly. 'I wonder if you would be so kind as to take me to a quiet, clean, reasonably priced hotel?'

'Central? Downtown? About fifteen to eighteen bucks a night?'

'That would do fine.'

It was really too expensive. He had budgeted for no more than twelve dollars a night.

'OK. I know a good quiet place. Could be less than fifteen bucks.'

'Thank you.'

'Going to be here long?'

'Just a few days.'

'You from England?'

'Scotland.'

'Same thing.'

He let that pass. He was fascinated by the man's assurance, by his taking it for granted that in spite of his black skin, thick lips, and inferior racial status he was as human as anybody else.

'Give you a piece of advice, if you want to take it. This place I'm taking you to is respectable, but lots of places downtown ain't. Rap parlours. Porno movies. Clip joints. Topless bars. Winos. Hookers. So keep off the streets after dark. Stay in your room and watch TV. Even if it's only Johnny Carson.' He laughed.

Robert laughed too, though he had never heard of Johnny Carson.

The hotel was called the Cabrillo. It was in a quiet street, next to a big bank. The foyer was carpeted. No disreputable characters were hanging about. The clerk at the desk was white.

The room was sixteen dollars a night, plus tax; but it had its own bathroom and telephone.

He sat on his bed and wondered what he should do. All during the long journey he had kept telling himself he shouldn't have come. He muttered it again, aloud.

At home he had left a mess; the shop up for sale, Marian gone to her sister in Aberdeen on the verge of a nervous breakdown, the two boys looking after themselves, and the whole town sniggering.

In front of him was a still worse mess; Cathie's husband and his relatives to meet, and the baby to be faced, not just as a repugnant idea but a living human being related to him.

He decided to wait till morning before telephoning. Her husband would be at work then. He had defied his superiors when he had married Cathie, just as she had defied her parents. He was said to have a beard and to be handsome,

158

for a black. He was only twenty-four. His name was Johnson. If he had been white he would have made an admirable son-in-law.

Next morning he was awakened by the sun shining through the curtains. Looking out, he saw with dismay streets bright with sunshine. He would have preferred grey skies and rain. Where could shame hide in all this brightness?

He waited till after nine. He had Cathie's letter in front of him with the telephone number on it. With stumbling finger he turned the dial.

A voice spoke, a woman's, surprisingly warm and pleasant.

'Lieutenant Johnson's residence,' she said.

His mouth was dry. 'Could I speak to Mrs Johnson, please?'

'I am Mrs Johnson. Who is calling?'

She must be Johnson's mother. His insides tightened with rage and resentment at his lovely fair-haired daughter being in the clutches of blacks with ugly faces and pleasant voices.

He put down the telephone. He wept. It was Marian's fault, she should have taken better care of her only daughter. No, it was his fault, he had let Cathie have her own way too much. It was the world's fault for having such mean, cruel prejudices.

He wondered what Mrs Johnson looked like.

Cathie would know now that he had come. His accent would have given him away. She would be waiting for him to telephone again or call in person at the house.

Was it possible that he had spent all that money and come all that way just to make one short abortive telephone call? That he could go home again without having seen her or without knowing if she had had her baby? Yes, it was. His love for Cathie might not prove stronger than his revulsion at her sweet white body being ravished and made pregnant by a black.

He checked himself. That was an evil thought.

He had always tried in his simple way to be fair to his fellow men. If a problem was too deep and complex for him he was never too proud to say so. He willingly left such matters to people better qualified. Here though was a problem of infinite difficulty that he must deal with himself. No one could help him. He might not be able to deal with it but surely he could do better than torment himself with vicious thoughts?

He wouldn't telephone, he would go in person. If he had to meet blacks what of it? They couldn't knife him. He would talk like a father to Cathie, lovingly and sensibly, pointing out that time healed or at least made hurts more bearable. If she had had her baby he would, if it couldn't be avoided, take it in his arms for a minute or two, as a grandfather should.

4

This time the taxi-driver was white, thank God. Robert asked him to stop a little distance from the house.

'Sure. That's easy. It's a condo. I'll drop you at the entrance. OK?'

'What's a condo?'

'Condominium. Sort of common ownership.'

'I see.'

He was in a foreign country where they did things differently. It made his mission all the more difficult.

When he was paying his hand shook. He felt sick. He had hardly eaten any breakfast.

'Have a good day,' said the driver.

Robert had already noticed this casual benevolence of Americans. Perhaps some of them meant it.

At the entrance was an arch of iron work with the words CANYON GROVE. Beside it was a notice warning that trespassers would be prosecuted. He wondered how they distinguished between trespassers and legitimate visitors.

The houses were painted white and two-storeyed. They didn't have gardens, only patios. But then the whole place was like a garden, with lawns, flowers, shrubs, and trees. It was all very well-kept. He noticed a swimming-pool, tennis courts, and a children's playground. In the midst of the houses was a wooded hollow: this must be the canyon.

The people who lived here must be comfortably off, but perhaps not rich enough to be above prejudice. If a rich black man like a film star married a white girl the rich people they associated with would accept it. Money in large enough quantities bought tolerance.

He wondered if Cathie's neighbours were unfriendly to her.

The number he was looking for was 6160. He saw it over a car-port. The car beneath was red, large, and quite new, a Buick. The house itself was approached along a paved path across a lawn. He had to keep moving, otherwise he might be regarded as a trespasser. He could count four dogs barking, probably at him. Luckily they were tied up in their patios.

As he lifted the latch of the gate and knocked on the door he asked himself, in an attempt at self-derogatory humour, what he was afraid of. They weren't cannibals. His worst ordeal would be having to be polite to them. He should be able to do it successfully enough. No one he knew would be present to wink or sneer or feel sorry for him. No one but Cathie.

161

As he waited, staring at a strange butterfly on a strange orange flower, he felt that all this wasn't real, he was dreaming it.

The door opened. There, smiling whitely at him, was a creature of dreamland.

Her face with its very dark colour and softness reminded him of tulips he had had in his garden once, with petals more black than purple and like silk to touch.

She was tall with shining jet-black hair. Her body was voluptuous. It gave off an exciting perfume. She wore a red blouse and yellow slacks.

'Good morning, Mr Nairn,' she said. 'Catherine was hoping you would call.'

She was the woman who had spoken to him on the telephone, Cathie's mother-in-law.

'Please come in,' she said. 'Catherine will be delighted to see you.'

They had never called Cathie Catherine.

He went in. There was no funny animal smell, as he had stupidly been expecting. Instead there was a fragrance of flowers. Everywhere was pink carpet, all over the floor and up the stairs.

On the stairs Cathie was standing. She looked as if she had just got out of bed. Under a white smock her belly was huge. Her face was pale, with big red blotches. Her mouth quivered, like an ill-done-to child's.

'I'm Celia Johnson,' said the tall black woman, 'Catherine's mother-in-law.'

She held out her hand. The palm was pinkish.

He hesitated, afraid that a handshake would be taken as a surrender of his right to protest, and afraid too of the effect on him of touching her.

She withdrew her hand, smiling. She had too much humour or sympathy to be offended.

162

'You'll want to talk to your daughter, Mr Nairn,' she said. 'I'll make myself busy upstairs.'

As she passed Cathie she kissed her on the cheek. 'Don't worry, honey. It's going to be all right.'

Cathie came down the stairs. He should have taken her in his arms, but he didn't. He just held out his hand, uselessly.

She sat on a couch. 'Why didn't you shake hands with Celia, Dad?' she asked, in a sad, weary voice. 'If it had been Mum I would have understood.'

'Don't talk like that about your mother,' he muttered.

What was wrong with him? Why was he being so surly? He wanted to be at his best. Only by showing love, forgiveness, and courage would he be able to help her.

'I'm sorry. I'll apologise to Mrs Johnson.'

'No. That would just make it worse. Celia understands. She's wonderful. Why don't you sit down, Dad?'

He sat down, reluctantly. He still didn't know if this was her home or Mrs Johnson's.

'How are you keeping, Cathie?' He wanted his voice to be loving and kind but he couldn't keep a girn out of it.

'I'm all right. I'm due any day now, as you can see. I've missed you all. How are the boys?'

'Fine. They're both fine. They send their love.'

She smiled. 'Do they?'

He hesitated. 'I'd to tell you they'll come and see you some day.'

'Silly things.' She was in tears but he saw that she was greatly encouraged.

'You said in your letter that you were afraid. Are people here nasty to you?'

He was ashamed to ask it. The people who had been most nasty to her had been her own father and mother.

'No. Most people are very nice. Why didn't Mum come?'

So in spite of everything she preferred her mother. He felt aggrieved.

'She didn't feel up to the journey. She's not been keeping well.'

'I'm sorry. I thought the boys would have written. Were they told not to?'

'Your mother made them promise. Anyway boys their age don't write many letters.'

'That's true. When did you arrive, Dad?'

'Last night.'

'Was it you that telephoned this morning?'

'Yes.'

'Where are you staying?'

'At a hotel called the Cabrillo.'

'We've got plenty of room here. I'll be going into hospital and Theo's at sea. Celia would look after you.'

His heart jumped. He wouldn't mind being looked after by Celia.

'Is this her house?' he asked.

'No, it's mine. Hers is bigger than this.'

'What does her man do?'

'He was a doctor.'

'What kind of doctor?'

'A medical doctor. He died two years ago.'

So Celia was a widow and slept alone.

'She's got two daughters. They're at Berkeley University, near San Francisco. They're beautiful and clever, like her.'

Looking at Cathie's pale blotched unhappy face and lustreless hair, he realised for the first time that from the blacks' point of view she might not be all that attractive.

All his life he had assumed that blacks were inferior to whites. So they were of course, in most things. But not always, it seemed, in physical beauty. Few white women were more beautiful than big Celia.

164

No, he wouldn't mind being looked after by her.

'That's Theo,' said Cathie, proudly.

He had already noticed the big coloured photograph but had kept avoiding it. Now he had to study it. Johnson did not look particularly Negroid, but then his beard hid his lips.

When white mated with black why was it always the black's characteristics that predominated in the offspring? It showed how cruel nature was. Cathie's child could be coal-black, with flat nose, thick lips, and crinkly hair. He would never be brave enough to hold it in his arms if anyone was watching.

He wouldn't mind holding Celia.

Cathie began to weep, quietly.

His blood turned cold. There was nothing he could do or say to comfort her. He could not say, 'It's all right, Cathie,' because it wasn't all right, or 'Never mind,' because she ought to mind, having destroyed her family's happiness, or 'It'll soon pass,' because with the birth of the child, and the births of other children, it would still be going on when he was in his grave.

Celia came down the stairs.

The way she walked, the way she held her arms, excited him.

Love was hard, lust easy.

She sat beside Cathie and put her arms round her. She looked at him not with contempt but with pity.

Cathie was sobbing that she wanted her mother.

Again he could not help feeling aggrieved. Nobody wanted him.

'I think you should go upstairs and lie down for a little while, honey,' said Celia. 'I'll make your father some tea.'

Cathie let herself be helped off the couch and up the stairs.

He forced himself to look again at his son-in-law's picture.

165

How did Johnson, as a black officer, get on in the Navy? Did the white ratings take orders from him in the same way that they did from white officers? Behind his back did they call him a coon? Did other blacks regard him as a traitor in that he was a willing part of the system that in their opinion oppressed them? Did he hope to rise higher than lieutenant?

He was doing what he had vowed never to do. He was showing interest in his son-in-law.

There was another photograph, of the two Johnson girls. Their lips were thick but their smiles were eager and their eyes bright.

Why were there no photographs of Cathie's own family?

Celia came down the stairs again. She would have suited the long gaudy robes of Africa.

'She'll sleep for a little while,' she said. 'First babies are always a great strain.'

Especially this first baby, he thought.

He couldn't keep his eyes off her as she went into the kitchen. In the tight yellow pants her backside was the most enticing he had ever seen, and in his day he had looked with wistful lust at many.

It was Marian's fault. In more than one way she had stripped him of his manliness. From the very first night she had looked on love-making as an irksome disgusting duty, to be done in the dark, briefly, and never talked about.

For months he had hated the very idea of black skin, and yet here he was fascinated by it, wanting to stroke it, smell it, kiss it.

She sat on the couch. Between them was a small table with the tea things on it.

'It's a pity Catherine's mother couldn't come,' she said, as she poured the tea.

'There was nothing to stop her. She just refused.'

He found pleasure in blaming Marian. It was like putting his hand down inside Celia's blouse. Were her nipples pink, like the tips of her fingers?

'I'm sorry. Catherine misses her very much.'

'She's sworn never to see her again. On the Bible.'

'She'll change her mind.'

'Will she? Do you know, she wanted me to tear up Cathie's letter without reading it? I wouldn't. So she just walked out of the house. That was about a fortnight ago. She's with her sister in Aberdeen. She's made herself ill. A nervous breakdown.'

If he had been exposing himself physically he would have felt the same guilty pleasure.

'She said that if I came here she'd never speak to me again. I don't understand her. We've been married over twenty years and I didn't know she was like that. It just shows you. I'm left with no one.'

'Haven't you got two boys, Mr Nairn?'

'Bob and Alistair. Yes. But they're just boys. They're not good at showing sympathy. They won't talk about their sister.'

Not to him. He suspected that they talked a great deal about her when they were alone.

'My son and I wanted to send you the money for your fare, Mr Nairn, but Catherine thought you might be offended.'

He grinned. 'When you're in my position you can't afford to be offended.'

'Excuse me, please.'

She got up and went over to a desk. From one of the drawers she took out a cheque-book.

'Is your first name Robert?' she asked.

He nodded. He imagined himself in bed with her, both of them naked. He wouldn't mind her being black then. In fact it would add to his enjoyment.

She wrote on the cheque, tore it out, and brought it
to him.

It was for a thousand dollars and was signed Celia Johnson.

'What's this for?' he muttered, remembering he was a white
man, with a white man's pride.

'To help with your expenses, Mr Nairn.'

The cheque was in his hand. 'I don't want your money.'

For the first time scorn was in her face and voice. 'What
do you want?'

'You,' he could have said, 'you, you big beautiful black
bitch.' What he did say was, 'You know what I want. I want
to take my daughter back home with me.'

She didn't believe him. He had never been any good at
telling lies, not because he loved the truth too much but
because he was too shallow.

'Let me tell you, Mrs Johnson, I think your son did a
terrible thing marrying my girl the way he did.'

'I quite agree with you, Mr Nairn.'

He was taken aback.

She lowered her voice. 'I didn't want this marriage, any
more than you and your wife did. I would have stopped
it if I could. It has caused my son a lot of trouble. It
might ruin his career. But it's done now and a baby's
coming. So their families, his and hers, must give them
every help.'

'I've told you my wife says she never wants to see her
again.'

'No mother in the world could keep that up, especially
when there's a baby involved.'

'The baby makes it worse. Maybe if there wasn't a baby –.'
But there was and it would be followed by others.

'What about you, Mr Nairn? Do you think the baby makes
it worse?'

He had to nod. If they had all been on a desert island it

168

would have been different, but they were in a world where people knew him.

'If that's your attitude I'm surprised you came.' She was scornful again, 'All you've done is break Catherine's heart all over again. I think you should go now.'

'I didn't come all this way just to talk to my daughter for two or three minutes.'

'All what way, Mr Nairn? You have made no journey that I can see. You are still in the same place where you always were.'

'That's ridiculous.'

Surely she knew Scotland was thousands of miles away. She might be a doctor's widow and have a marvellous body but she was black and therefore not as intelligent as he, who was white.

'All you have done is to make her feel more guilty and more unhappy.'

'She didn't say that. You're putting words into her mouth.'

Suddenly she looked fierce, like one of her savage ancestors. She pressed her face close to his. Her breath was spicy.

'I'll tell you what she did say, Mr Nairn. She said that you and your wife would be pleased if she died having the baby, and if the baby died too.'

He jumped to his feet. He wasn't going to sit there and be insulted by this big she-ape, even if she was speaking the truth. He had a good mind to punch her on the fat mouth.

He pushed the cheque into his pocket. Why shouldn't he be compensated? It was her son's fault that he had had to put himself in debt.

He would come back when Cathie was a bit recovered. They would order this woman out of the house. They had a right as father and daughter to talk in private.

'I'm sorry, Mr Nairn,' she said. 'I truly am sorry.'

Under his breath he muttered 'Keep your fucking pity,' but he would have loved her to take him in her arms and comfort him. 'I'll be back,' he said.

She shook her head. She knew that he didn't have the compassion or the courage to come back.

Outside on the paved path he had to step aside as a small child on a tricycle came towards him.

'Hi,' she said.

He could tell she was a girl from her pigtails tied with red ribbons. She had merry eyes but she was black to the ear-tips, with a tinge of yellow.

Goodbye Phoenix, Arizona

1

NOBODY WHO KNEW THEM was much surprised when it was learned that Annie Baxter and Bella McMurtrie, who had just won £8,596.45 on the football pools, were going to spend a part of it (squander it most people thought) on a trip to Las Vegas. For, respectable widows though they were, in their fifties, they were compulsive gamblers. Four times a week they went to Bingo. Often they paid quick sly visits to the betting shop in Selkirk Street. They bought tickets for every raffle going, whether the prize was a motor bicycle or a case of whisky. They had stood and delivered to every one-armed bandit in the town, especially the one in the bowling club, where other members grumbled about their monopolising it. And of course they filled in football coupons religiously every week.

Not all gamblers, however addicted, would have had the boldness or extravagance to go on a pilgrimage to Las Vegas, their Mecca, in a country where murders and rapes were ten a penny, but then, Annie and Bella, belying their demure appearance, were high-spirited, gallous, and idiosyncratic ladies. For instance, one Hallowe'en, two or three years back, they had gone out guising, although most children had given up the practice as old-fashioned. Faces blackened, lips whitened, and wearing frock coats and top hats borrowed from the Oxfam shop, they had gone round their friends' houses, singing and dancing like minstrels, in return for nuts and apples.

Not everyone in the town found their antics amusing. Some women of their own age or older called them a disgrace. A favourite male opinion, often expressed at the bowling club bar when no ladies were present, and sometimes on the hallowed green itself, was that what big Annie and wee Bella needed to rein them in a bit were men in their beds again.

It was admitted, even by the one or two who didn't like them, that their flightiness never took the form of fornication. Like many other Scottish church-going widows of their generation they enjoyed a randy joke now and then but were resolutely chaste, which on the whole was as it should be, for they had loved their husbands and had been married in church, therefore though nobody expected them to wear black all the time it was considered quite proper that they should remain single, like widowed swans.

Annie was tall, slim, and silver-haired; Bella small and plump, with hair kept chestnut coloured by assiduous tinting.

They lived in different parts of the town, Annie in a flat she owned, and Bella in a council house.

Annie's husband, Jack, an engineer, had died of cirrhosis of the liver, at the age of forty-seven, against all the odds for he had been a teetotaller. Her daughter, Jean, had emigrated to New Zealand where she was now matron of a hospital. They wrote to each other regularly.

Bella's man, Arthur, a joiner, had died of lung cancer. He had been forty-five and a non-smoker. Her son Dick, also a joiner, now lived in Toronto as a naturalised Canadian. He was married to a woman who, judging by the one photograph he sent, was half Chinese and at least ten years older than he. Bella wrote to him twice a year, once at Christmas and once on his birthday. She had got used to getting no reply. She knew that Dick hated writing letters and she suspected that his wife didn't know enough English. They had two children whom she had never seen.

Both their husbands had died in the same week, in the same hospital, on a cold wet December ten years ago.

It was noticed that though they were known to many and frequently talked about no one knew them all that well. Who had seen them sad? Who had heard them weep? A woman herself a widow, who had accompanied them to the cemetery to put flowers on their husbands' graves reported that, while she herself had shed tears, they had cracked jokes.

2

They were granted three weeks leave from their jobs on condition they provided replacements. This was easy for they had many obliging friends. Indeed the headmaster of the primary school where Bella worked in the canteen went out of his way to accommodate her. A man of sixty-two with a skinny peevish wife he often wished he could exchange her for cuddly cheerful Mrs McMurtrie.

Annie was manageress of a baker's shop. Its owner, Donald Gilliespie, had once proposed to her. That she had turned him down puzzled some and displeased a few. Just who did big Annie think she was? Though no oil painting Donald had a prosperous business and a detached villa, called Achnamara. She had said, at the bowling club, with the straightest of faces, that it wasn't comfort and safety she was looking for but romance and adventure.

Their trip was arranged by Archie Kintyre, the only travel agent in town. They were to fly to Las Vegas via Los Angeles. A double room had been reserved for them in the Meteor Hotel, on the famous Strip. Going against his own interests

Archie had tried to persuade them to choose some place less expensive, not so far away, and not so dangerous for ladies on their own. He warned them that things were allowed in Nevada that were banned in other American States. What things they had asked, innocently. A man of little humour he had not realised that they were teasing him, for they were good at keeping their faces straight. Did he mean brothels? They themselves had always believed that if brothels were legal there would be fewer cases of rape. Didn't he agree? Behind his big dour face had flickered for a few moments the suspicion that they were going to that wicked city not only to gamble but to misbehave in other ways too. He was tempted to tell them that they stood no chance, Las Vegas being full of beautiful young whores.

On their way back they were to spend a few days in Los Angeles visiting Disneyland and the Universal Studios where, they said, they might bump into Robert Redford or Telly Savalas.

All the same most people, though admiring their enterprise and envying their escaping three weeks of Scottish winter, thought that they would have done better to spend the money on visiting their children.

It wasn't the first time they had flown. They had been to Torremolinos in the south of Spain several times. Annie had found that she did not like flying, Bella that she loved it. Therefore as they flew over Greenland's icy mountains Bella jauntily hummed the hymn tune, while Annie, eyes closed, groaned.

'That was old Mr Chisolm's favourite hymn,' said Bella. 'He was superintendent of the Sunday school. Big flat-footed man with skelly eyes.'

'What church was this?'

'St John's.'

'It was St Cuthbert's Sunday school I went to.'

'We dirty-minded lassies used to say his eyes got skelly with trying to peep down Miss McDonald's blouse. She had a gorgeous figure. Old Mr Chisolm's son, Andrew, was killed in the war. His plane crashed.'

'Let's change the subject, if you don't mind.'

'Sorry, Annie.'

Bella smiled and let herself dream. If she got the chance of an affair with some big-time gambler why shouldn't she take it? No one need ever know, not even Annie. It might do Annie good to have a wee fling herself.

In Torremolinos once, reckless and light-headed with too much wine, Bella had let herself be led by a Spaniard with brown eyes and grey sideburns into a narrow alley, where in moonlight with someone playing a guitar nearby and with geraniums scenting the air, he had shoved her against a knobbly whitewashed wall and had her dress up and her pants halfway down before the reek of garlic off his breath brought her back to earth. She had pushed him off and returned more or less unravished to the bar, where Annie for a while had refused to speak to her.

At Los Angeles International Airport Annie felt exhausted and seedy, so it was energetic Bella who identified their suitcases on the moving platform, found a taxi, instructed the driver to take them to the terminal for internal flights, and got them safely on the plane for Las Vegas.

They arrived in the gloaming. Below were deserts and stony mountains, pink with sunset. Then suddenly there were tall buildings, blue swimming pools, green golf courses, and twinkling lights.

A pilgrim arriving at Lourdes, hopeful of miracles, could not have looked down with greater wonder than Bella.

'Wake up, Annie. We're here.'

'Where's here? Hell?'

'No. Heaven. Las Vegas. Hallelujah.'

In the airport building they saw the first of the legions of one-armed bandits.

Driving along the famous Strip the taxi-driver pointed out hotels and casinos like Caesar's Palace and Stardust.

Half an hour later they were in their own hotel, the Meteor, in their own air-conditioned room. To reach it they had walked through the huge carpeted casino. Not only its size had reminded them of a church.

Kicking off her shoes and whispering that she was fair wabbit Annie lay down on one of the beds.

Bella explored. She tried the TV set to see if it was black and white or coloured, it was coloured. In the bathroom she was amused by the paper band sealing the lavatory seat.

'We've got to remember,' she said, as she too lay down, 'that we're in a foreign country, even if they do speak the same language.'

'Not altogether the same,' murmured Annie. 'They call Bingo Keno.'

'And they don't say pontoon, they say blackjack.'

'And Zee for Zed.'

They both laughed. It had been for these and other differences that they had come all that way, as well as of course for the gambling.

3

Later that evening, bathed, perfumed, and very smart in their new trouser suits, Bella's off-white and Annie's pale-blue, they set out for their first taste of nocturnal Las Vegas. Since they were still suffering from jet lag they intended that night to stick to their own hotel and casino. There would be plenty of other nights on which to visit more famous places like Caesar's Palace, Sands, and Desert Inn.

In the restaurant a buffet dinner was being offered for $3.95, as much as you could eat. They did not feel hungry so they went into the coffee shop where, while they were deciding what to order, a Mexican with a black moustache came and poured out coffee without being asked. Bella, however, wanted tea. 'Hot tea?' he asked. 'Hot tea,' she replied, wondering who could be so daft as to want it cold. He brought it in a small silver-plated pot with a tea-bag and a slice of lemon. She had to ask for milk.

Americans, it seemed, drank their tea or coffee before they ate. What could be more foreign than that?

Annie ordered fish and French fries, for safety's sake. Bella boldly chose a pattimelt, without ever having seen one.

It turned out to be a round of hamburger meat with soapy cheese melted on it, all on top of a hunk of rye bread. It was tasty enough, she conceded, but you needed elastic jaws to eat it.

The other occupants of the coffee shop were a disappointment. They were mostly respectable elderly American couples. It was possible to play Keno while you ate, but not many were doing it. Perhaps, suggested Bella, they were saving their nickels for the fruit machines. They looked as if it would be the nickel machines they would play. They had come to Las Vegas to gamble but not recklessly. The big-time gamblers would eat in more expensive places than this.

In the casino it was warm and comfortable. The change girls wore red dresses that showed off their fine bosoms and shapely thighs. One was black, tall, and beautiful. Bella wasn't surprised to notice that some of the hardened gamblers playing blackjack or poker or craps lifted their heads to look at her.

There were hundreds of machines, row upon row of them. They looked friendly and encouraging with their bright twinkling lights. Now and then bells rang and coins cascaded into metal boxes as someone was lucky.

As ex-pupils of Scottish Sunday schools Bella and Annie would have been the first to agree that to put a nickel in a slot, pull a handle, watch the roller spinning, as often as not to no avail, insert another coin as instructed, and do it all over again, as many times as you had nickels or dimes or quarters was as silly and empty a way of passing an evening as could be imagined. Nevertheless they found it enthralling.

Bella's fifteenth attempt had the bell ringing and nickels spewing out, two hundred of them. She changed them into quarters and moved on to try the quarter machines.

As for Annie, she was bolder still. After half an hour of trying the machines she decided to have a go at blackjack. An hour later she was winning twenty-five dollars.

They gave up at quarter past two. They could hardly keep their eyes open. Annie was thirteen dollars to the good, Bella three.

Before leaving they had a shot each at the big dollar machine. Both lost.

They crept off to bed then, confident that they were going to enjoy their escapade in Las Vegas.

Creeping down the corridor to their room, quietly, so as not to disturb anyone who might be asleep, they saw a young woman, with dyed blonde hair and purple lips, coming out of a room. She passed them stinking of scent. They smiled but she hurried past, head in the air.

'Give you three guesses,' said Bella.

'One's enough.'

'But isn't this supposed to be a respectable hotel?'

'We're in Las Vegas, remember.'

'Should we complain to the management?'

'Do you think she gets double time, working such late hours?'

'I wonder who her customer was.'

'Room 91, wasn't it? We'll keep our eyes open.'

'Maybe we could do a little business ourselves.'

'We might have to if our luck runs out.' They managed to reach their own room before shrieking with laughter.

4

They never found out who Miss Purple-Lips' customer was, but they did learn, from a newssheet given out free, that it was possible in Las Vegas to hire what were called 'touch escorts'. What touching involved could be easily imagined. According to the advertisements they all had health certificates. What convulsed Bella and Annie was that, in smaller print, it mentioned that male escorts were also available. They had some ribald fun imagining what would happen if they were to pick up the telephone one night and ask for two escorts as virile as Clint Eastwood to be sent to their room.

That first morning, after a long lie in bed, they visited Caesar's Palace and were much impressed by its opulence. They took each other's photograph standing by the headless angel outside, and Julius Caesar himself inside. In the Ladies' they marvelled at how sumptuous it was. Above the door it said 'Cleopatra's'. Above the Gents' it said 'Caesars'.

They decided that Caesar's Palace was for the rich. It didn't make them feel cheap, not even Buckingham Palace would have done that, but it made them realise that only if they kept within their limits would they be able to enjoy themselves. It was all very well their telling each other that in these imperial premises they might at any moment bump into Frank Sinatra or Dean Martin, not wearing togas or laurel wreaths exactly, but still gleaming with the patina and insolence of wealth. They knew that those celebrated gentlemen wouldn't have given them a second weary glance. If they were to have fun and pleasure it must be with people as ordinary as themselves.

In the afternoon they paid a visit to the Wee Kirk Among the Heather and watched an instant wedding taking place, with a fat bride and a big-eared groom. Though the ceremony was silly and made them laugh, Bella couldn't help feeling solemn too. Indeed she had tears in her eyes. She remembered her own wedding, more than thirty years ago, in St John's Church, with her Calum wearing a kilt. That had been, she now realised, the happiest and proudest moment of her life.

But Las Vegas was not the place for sacred memories. Though she had been there for less than forty-eight hours she had already seen that only money was worshipped there and human feelings, unless one was very careful, soon turned hard.

On the fourth day Annie went into one of her sulks.

They were in their own casino playing the machines when, suddenly, without a word, she walked away, her face grim and haughty.

Bella had seen it coming. She had been snapped at several times. What caused these moods in Annie she had never been able to find out. Some deep indissoluble disappointment, maybe. She knew better than to run after her and offer comfort. Annie wanted no one's company at such times.

Feeling forsaken, Bella went on playing the machines, but her heart wasn't in it, it seemed such a useless empty pastime. So at last she went into the bar for a drink before going to bed.

She sat on a high stool at the counter and ordered a Scotch. There weren't many people present, only a few morose losers.

He spoke twice before she realised he was addressing her. 'Where's your friend?'

She turned round.

He was small, skinny, white-haired, and sad-looking, dressed in a ridiculous evening suit with glittering lapels, not at all suitable for a man his age, which was at least sixty.

'She's gone to bed,' she said, curtly. She was in no mood to be picked up, especially by someone like him.

He persisted. 'Wasn't she feeling well?'

'She felt tired, that's all.'

'I saw her leave suddenly, as if she felt ill.'

So he had been spying on them or rather on Annie.

'Do you mind if I join you?' he asked.

'You've already done, haven't you?'

'Can I order you another drink?'

'No thanks. As soon as this is finished I'm off to bed.'

'May I ask where you are from? You speak as if you're from Scotland.'

'I am. So's Annie.'

'Annie? Is that her name? She's a very handsome woman.'

Did she feel a pang of jealousy? If she did it was stupid.

'Are you here on vacation?'

'You could say that.'

'Am I right in thinking you are both widows?'

'You are. Merry widows. Where are you from yourself?'

'Phoenix, Arizona.'

Arizona she connected with cowboys. She couldn't imagine him on a horse.

'Have you been in Vegas long?' he asked.

'Four days.'

'I arrived yesterday.'

'In Arizona do you own a ranch?'

She meant it as a joke. He took it seriously. That was the kind of old creep he was. Not her sort at all, or Annie's.

'I am manager of a supermarket.'

181

She imagined him galloping along the aisles on a trolley. She managed not to smile. 'Is this your first visit to Las Vegas?' she asked.

'My second. The last was twenty years ago.'

'It's our first and last.'

'Why, aren't you enjoying yourselves? I may say you've looked as if you were.'

'It's all right but it's very far away and it's very expensive.'

'My wife was with me last time.'

'Didn't she want to come this time? Lots of people wouldn't care for it.' Sensible people, too.

'She was buried three days ago.'

'Oh.' He had lost no time in getting to Vegas. Yet he didn't look a desperate gambler. 'I'm sorry to hear that.'

'Cancer. Cancer of the rectum.'

'My God!' The whisky suddenly tasted vile. 'I hope she didn't suffer too much.'

'It was pretty rough.'

'Have you any family?'

'Two sons and a daughter, all married.'

'Any grandchildren?'

'Eight.'

Tears came into her eyes. She had two whom she had never seen. In the one photograph that she had been sent they looked Chinese, but that wasn't the reason why she had never gone to see them. She hadn't been invited.

'They wanted me to go and live with them till I'd got over it.'

'You should have.'

'I guess I wanted to be by myself.'

She understood. If he had stayed at home he would have been tormented by memories of his wife. Everything in the house would have reminded him of her, even a stain on a

182

tablecloth. If he had gone to live with his family they would have overwhelmed him with their sympathy.

Wanting to be alone he had come to the right place. Gambling was greed and nothing separated people more than greed. She saw that clearly. She ought never to gamble again. She would but she shouldn't.

All the same, was he to be trusted? His story could be a pack of lies. Perhaps he had absconded with the supermarket's funds. Perhaps his wife had died of an axe through the skull. He looked harmless, but then wife-murderers often did.

'My name's Sampson, with a p. Herbert Sampson.'

She kept her face straight. Even with a p the name wasn't very appropriate. 'Mine's Isobel McMurtrie.'

'And your friend's?'

'Annie Baxter.'

He repeated it, in a whisper. It seemed to be a comfort to him. Did Annie remind him of his wife?

She wriggled off the stool. 'Well, Mr Sampson, I think I'll be off to my bed. Good night.'

'Good night, Isobel. Be sure and give my regards to Annie.'

As she made for her room she thought that this little adventure would be the very thing to cheer Annie up.

The room was in darkness, but she smelled cigarette smoke.

'I'm not asleep,' said Annie. 'Put on the light.'

Bella switched on the lamp by her bed.

Annie was lying in bed, smoking. She seemed to have got over her depression quickly this time. 'You look pleased with yourself,' she said. 'Did you win the jackpot?'

'I met somebody.'

'Do you mean somebody tried to pick you up?'

Taking off her clothes Bella turned her back to Annie. They were always very modest in front of each other.

183

'Who was he? A rich Arab, I hope.'

'A Yank, from Phoenix, Arizona.'

'Wearing a stetson and chewing baccy?'

'He manages a supermarket. So he said. I wasn't sure whether to believe him or not. He was more interested in you than in me.'

'Me?'

'It seems he's been admiring you from afar.'

'Is he married? Did he say?'

'A widower. His wife was buried three days ago. Cancer of the rectum.'

'Poor soul.'

'Him or her?'

'Him now. Did he just come up and speak to you?'

'Yes, in the bar.'

'What's he like? How old is he?'

'He's not like his name, that's for sure. He's wee and puny. You could pick him up and run away with him under your oxter. Herbert Sampson, with a p. All the time he was interested in you.'

'Has he got a car?'

'I don't know. He didn't say. Why?'

'If he has he could be very useful. There are lots of interesting places we could visit.'

'Not with him, thank you very much. He's creepy. You should have seen the jacket he was wearing. It was purple with black sparkling lapels.'

'Sparkling lapels!' Annie laughed. 'He sounds fun, Bella.'

'With his wife just newly dead? Even at the best of times I doubt if he ever laughed much.'

'Well, isn't it our Christian duty to help cheer the poor man up?'

'You can try if you like, Annie. Me, I'm for steering clear of him.'

5

Next morning they were in the coffee room eating scrambled eggs and pancakes with syrup when Herbert came in. He was wearing white trousers and a black jacket. He waved his hat at them. It was a white Panama.

'That him?' whispered Annie.

Bella nodded. 'Let's ignore him.'

'No. Wave to him. Invite him to join us.' Annie herself waved.

He almost ran over to their table. He had eyes only for Annie. Offered her hand, he took it and was reluctant to let go. She wasn't embarrassed but Bella was. Bella was indignant too. At home Annie had the reputation of being stand-offish, and yet here she was greeting this dubious wee man as if he and she were on intimate terms.

He had a car all right. Annie soon found that out. He was very proud of it. An Oldsmobile, only a year old; air-conditioned, electrically operated doors. Sure, he would be honoured to take them anywhere they wanted to go. The Boulder Dam. Lake Mead. The Spring mountains. As he chatted to Annie, Bella felt left out and let herself go into a huff. They discovered that they both liked swimming. Eager as children, or lovers, they arranged to have a swim in the heated pool, in an hour's time. Bella was included but she shook her head. Annie knew fine she couldn't swim. Besides in a swimming costume her fatness would be revealed, as would Annie's slimness.

They went to their room for Annie to change into her bathing costume.

'I thought we were going to tour the Mint Casino this morning,' said Bella.

'We can do that any time.'

Holding up her arms in front of the mirror Annie examined her oxters.

Bella hated to sound querulous but couldn't help it.

'What am I supposed to do while you're in the pool?'

'Come in with us.'

'You know I can't swim.'

'You could paddle.'

'I'm a bit old for paddling.'

'Well, you could sit by the pool and have a drink.'

'At this time in the morning? Thank you, but I'm not an alcoholic.'

'It's up to you.' Annie was now inspecting her breasts.

'About this trip to the mountains, were you serious?'

'Of course. We can't live in casinos all the time.'

'I thought that was what we came for.'

'We need some fresh air. Besides I'd like to see some of the countryside.'

'It's just desert and stony mountains. You know nothing about him, Annie. How do you know he'll not take you to some lonely canyon and cut your throat?'

'If you think that shouldn't you come along to protect me?'

'We've only got his word that his wife died of cancer. For all we know he could have murdered her.'

'Herbert's not got the nerve to be a murderer.'

'So it's Herbert already?'

'We're in America, Bella, where everybody uses first names.'

'There are people at home who've known you for thirty years and still call you Mrs Baxter.'

'We're on holiday, Bella, and we're in Las Vegas. If we're not going to have adventures here we never will have.'

'What sort of adventures do you have in mind, Annie?'

'Who can tell? Well, are you coming?'

'No, I am not. You don't really want me to come.'
'Don't be ridiculous.'
'I don't understand you, Annie.'
'Well, that's only fair. At times you're a mystery to me.'
'I'm flabbergasted.'
'How do I look?'
'Like a woman of fifty-six who thinks she's thirty again.'
'Jealousy doesn't become you, Bella. Are you coming?'
'No.'
'Toddle-loo then. See you later.'
Off she went, wrapped in a white towel.
The backs of her legs, Bella noted with spiteful satisfaction, were marred by varicose veins.

6

Feeling very ill-done by, Bella spent the whole day by herself. It wasn't easy. Crowded casinos were very lonely places. She took a taxi to Circus-Circus where she threw rings, propelled balls, and fired a gun, in attempts to win stuffed animals that she didn't want. She made faces in distorting mirrors. She watched acrobats.

After a solitary lunch in Denny's she took another taxi to downtown Las Vegas, where the escort agencies were and the cinemas showing pornographic movies. She was tempted to go into one of those, to be degraded just as Annie somewhere was being degraded. She felt unwanted and useless. She told herself several times she would never speak to Annie again.

But at six she hurried back eagerly to her room, hoping to find Annie there. Instead there was a note stuck to the dressing-table mirror. In it Annie said she was sorry to have missed Bella but she had been asked by Herbert to dinner and afterwards a show at the Stardust.

What kind of man was it, thought Bella, sorrier than ever for herself, who with his wife newly dead from a horrible disease took another woman who looked like her to a show where beautiful young girls danced naked? And what kind of a woman was it who encouraged him?

She spent the whole evening in her room, trying to find something interesting on television, and waiting for Annie.

The telephone rang just before midnight. Bella was in bed but not asleep.

'Is that you, Annie?' she asked, as if she didn't really care. But there were tears in her eyes.

'Aye, it's me. Just to let you know I'll not be back tonight.'

'You mean, you're spending the night with him?'

'That's right. I'm sorry about today, Bella. We went for a sail on Lake Mead. You should have come.'

'Wouldn't I have been in the way?'

'I'll see you in the morning.'

'At what time, may I ask?'

'At this moment I have no idea.'

'This isn't like you, Annie.'

'That's what I've been telling myself.'

'I'm shocked. I really am.'

'Good-night, Bella. I'm a bit shocked myself.'

Bella put the telephone down. Her tears flowed. 'You never know anybody,' she muttered.

The unfairness of the situation made it all the more painful. She was the one who'd often suggested that they ought to have discreet affairs, and Annie was the one who'd always rebuked her for it. She remembered Annie's sour face when she'd gone out of the bar with the lustful Spaniard in Torremolinos. Yet here was Annie letting herself be enticed into bed by an unknown gloomy-faced sixty-year-old Yank, just because he had a swanky car.

She didn't sleep well and was immediately awakened when, at half-past six, the door opened and Annie crept in, carrying her shoes.

'Asleep, Bella?' she whispered.

'I've not been asleep all night.'

'Sorry about that. Do you mind if I put on the light?'

'Do what you like.'

'I've got a lot to tell you, Bella, but maybe I should wait till later.'

Bella wanted to say that she didn't care if she was never told but she couldn't, it would have been too big a lie, her voice would have given her away. So she said nothing.

'Well, to get to the nub as they say, he's asked me to marry him.'

'He's not the first man to say that to a woman, hoping to get his way with her.'

'Herbert's not like that.'

'What *is* Herbert like? You said you don't understand me who's known you for thirty years, so how can you understand him whom you've hardly known for thirty hours?'

'He's easy to know. Transparent. Simple. Nice. Good-hearted. Obliging.'

'I wouldn't have thought a simpleton would be made manager of a supermarket in America.'

'He showed me photographs of Phoenix. A lovely town, Bella. He's got a fine big house.'

'Made of wood.'

'So it is, but that's the style there. Sunshine all the year round.'

'I've heard you say you'd hate that. You like snow and wind and rain now and then, I've heard you say that often.'

'But I'm getting old, Bella. My bones need warmth.'

'What about his family? Did he tell you about them?'

'He told me everything.'

189

'I can believe that, but how much of it was true? Americans do a lot of bragging.'

'Not Herbert. He's really humble.'

'He doesn't dress as if he was humble. I can't see you being happy amongst a crowd of American relatives.'

'Why do you say that?'

'Because you're an aloof kind of person. There are people at home who think you're stuck-up because you're so aloof. This is Bella McMurtrie talking, who's known you for thirty years. Did you give him an answer? Did you say you would?'

'I'm to tell him today.'

'And what are you going to tell him?'

'I don't know yet. I haven't made up my mind.'

'Well, don't ask for my advice. I'd rather keep out of it. But I will remind you that it would mean giving up all your friends to go and live among strangers.'

'You could come and stay with us, Bella, for as long as you liked. Herbert said so.'

'No, thank you. I think I've had enough of America.'

'Well, let's get some sleep.'

Bella hated herself for saying bitterly 'Why, didn't he let you get any?'

'As I said, he was telling me the story of his life.'

Bella hated herself even more for asking 'Well, did you or didn't you?'

'We did. But it wasn't much of a success. Maybe he was remembering his wife. It could get better, I expect. But I would never marry a man just for that.'

'Would you go home first and then come back?'

'He wants us to get married here in Las Vegas.'

'In the Wee Kirk Among the Heather?'

Annie laughed. 'He thinks it's very romantic.'

'Simple's right then.'

They went to sleep then or at any rate tried to. After some

angry anxious thoughts Bella dozed off. When she awoke about three hours later she found Annie sitting up in bed with a pack of cards in her hand.

It was a funny time to be playing patience.

But she wasn't. She was just holding the cards. She seemed to have been waiting for Bella to wake up.

'Hello,' she said. 'I need a witness.'

'What are you havering about?'

'I'm going to cut the cards.'

'What for?' Bella was still not fully alert.

'To find out what answer I should give Herbert.'

'You're not serious.'

'Oh, but I am. Whatever the cards say I'll stick to. You know me. I never cheat. But I'd like you to be a witness.'

Bella sat up, disapproving but fascinated. After all she was a gambler too.

'You see, Bella, I'd like to marry him, it would be an adventure, but I'd like just as much to go back home with you. That's why I can't decide.'

'Shouldn't you think about it a bit more? We're going to be here another eight days.'

'I've been thinking about it all night. I'll never be able to make up my mind, so I'll have to have it made up for me. The cards will do it. Would you like to cut them for me?'

'Sorry, Annie. I wouldn't like to think I was responsible.'

'But you wouldn't be. It would be fate.'

As devout gamblers they had often discussed the mysteries of fate.

'I suppose it would, Annie, but I'd still feel responsible.'

'Well then, I'll cut myself. Will you shuffle them?'

Bella couldn't object to that. She took the cards and shuffled them well. Then she handed them back. She felt in awe of Annie.

191

'My left hand is for saying no, I'll not marry him. My right hand is for saying yes, I will. Got that, Bella?'

'Yes, Annie, I've got that, but – ' Bella was about to point out that this method of deciding was not fair to Herbert, but she changed her mind. Why shouldn't Herbert be at the mercy of fate too?

With her left hand Annie cut. It was the five of spades, a card easily beaten. She showed it to Bella. 'I don't think they should be shuffled again, do you?'

Bella shook her head and watched as Annie, this time with her right hand, again cut the cards. Without hesitation she showed the card revealed. It was the four of diamonds. Fate had said no, but seemed to have had doubts too. The margin couldn't have been narrower.

'Well, that's that,' said Annie, cheerfully. 'Goodbye, Phoenix, Arizona.'

Bella had heard of gamblers staking a million dollars on the throw of dice, but it seemed to her that Annie's gamble had been more tremendous than that; she had risked her whole future.

She was now singing in the bathroom. That was how to accept fate's verdicts, with courage and cheerfulness.

All the same, poor Herbert.

She Had to Laugh

1

EVERY SATURDAY EVENING THE three of them met on the 5.30 pm train bound for the coast town where they would do their best to be picked up by American sailors off the USS *Canopus* in the Holy Loch. As whores they were amateurs, so much so that, though they would never have been so innocent as to admit it, they kept hoping, week-end after week-end, for some other reward than free drinks, chewing-gum, and a few dollars, romance for instance or even, for some of the sailors were raw lads from what the Americans called the boon-docks, offers of marriage.

They were from the East End of Glasgow where on and off they worked in factories at unskilled jobs. They knew that respectable people, particularly women, looked down on them as scruff and so they often acted and spoke more scruffily than they really wanted to, for they had their own standards. When speaking to one another their language was so dialectal as to be unintelligible to outsiders, so that they had to twist their tongues and curb their sense of humour in talking 'proper' for the benefit of their American friends, as they preferred to call them. It had also to be made less obscene, otherwise even those whoremongering sailors might have been shocked.

They spent much money and time on their appearance.

The results, in the eyes of respectable people, were ghastly, but in their own and in those of the less discriminating sailors, enchanting. They plastered on make-up with the lavishness of clowns. They wore long dresses of the gaudiest colours, plushy overcoats, spangly handbags, dangling earrings, rings as big as knuckledusters (they had to be removed when certain delicate services were called for) and silver or gold shoes with heels so high that they tottered rather than walked.

Only Tessa, the oldest at twenty and a half, had to wear a padded bra. The other two, Sadie and Cissie, did not need one, Cissie especially, for she had very big breasts. Tessa's legs too were the skinniest and her teeth the most decayed. Yet she was the one most often picked up and paid more than the customary ten dollars, so good was she at giving satisfaction.

Because they were drunk or were thinking of wives back home or because of both these reasons combined sailors were often impotent or what was worse semi-impotent. Many a difficult half-hour had Sadie and Cissie, in bushes in the public gardens or in shop doorways or in the backs of cars, with no reward at the finish or rather at the lack of finish. That never happened to Tessa. (Even if it was made of plasticine, Sadie once said wistfully, Tessa could get it stiff.)

She was the kind of woman who in the past could have become a king's or a cardinal's mistress and held the office for many years, ending up with a fortune and a title. The boon she had to bestow was the one men were most grateful for.

Even so Sadie and Cissie were incredulous one wet June evening when Tessa read out to them in the train bits of a letter she had received that morning from America. She showed them the Californian postmark. It contained a proposal of marriage. More astounding still were the four 50-dollar bills that she said had come with it. They believed her. She was no liar or boaster. The Yank had written that if

194

she was willing to come to Anglia and be his wife he would send another 200 dollars for her air fare to Los Angeles, where he would meet her.

'Who the hell is he?' asked Cissie, awed and envious. 'Can you mind him, Tessa?'

'Sure. Harry Folger. He left about six months ago. He sent his photie in case I'd forgotten him.'

She took it out of her handbag.

Her friends looked at it. He was no Robert Redford. His ears were too big, he had a glaikit grin, his eyes were small and close together, and his shoulders were narrow. But he was male and he lived in California.

'Whit was he like, as a bloke?' asked Sadie.

'A' right. Very generous.'

'Did he ever say onything aboot wanting to mairry you while he was here?'

'He did. I never took him seriously.'

'Could he manage it?' sneered Cissie. 'Did he need help? He looks it.'

'He needed help but he could manage it.'

'Don't heed us, Tessa,' said Sadie. 'She's jealous. Like me.'

'This place Anglia,' said Cissie, 'I never heard of it. Whaur is it?'

'California.'

'California's a big place.'

'Does it matter?' asked Sadie.

Even Cissie had to agree that it didn't. All California was sunny. All Californians were well-off and tanned. California was paradise.

'It cannae be a big place,' said Tessa. 'I looked in an auld school atlas but couldnae find it.'

'It must be near the sea, him being a sailor,' said Cissie.

'He's left the Navy. He didnae like it.'

195

'Whit does he dae noo?'

'He's inherited his faither's gas filling station and store.'

'Did his faither dee?' asked Sadie.

'Four weeks ago.'

'You're lucky, Tessa,' said Sadie. 'We'll miss you, but you should go. I would.'

'I'm thinking about it, Sadie.'

'If that's so,' said Cissie, 'why are you coming wi' us the night?'

Tessa patted her hand. Their bracelets clinked together. 'Once I've gi'en him my word, Cissie, if I gie it that's to say, I'll no' let anither man touch me, for the rest of my life.'

'That's a laugh,' said Sadie, sadly.

2

Although she could find no one to tell her where Anglia was and what sort of place it was, Tessa decided that wherever it was and whatever it was like it was bound to be better than the street of condemned tenements where she lived with her mother, her half-sister Roberta, and her half-brother Billy. Roberta was fourteen and Billy twelve. They did not know who their fathers were. Their mother wasn't quite a prostitute, she was just too willing to let men into her bed. Tessa had first seen the male organ at the ready when she was only three. She sometimes thought that was the reason she never found it fearsome. The man about to throw himself on top of her mother had a few minutes before given her a poke of sweeties and a doll with a china face.

She wrote to Harry saying that she would be pleased to marry him if he sent the rest of the money. The letter took her hours to write. She sought no one's help.

During the weeks of waiting for a reply she kept going

with Sadie and Cissie to Lunderston. She did not yet consider herself betrothed.

At last came the reply. Harry did not say much about Anglia but he sent the money.

She wrote at once thanking him and telling him she would let him know as soon as possible the date and time of her arrival in Los Angeles.

To obtain a passport she had to fill in a form and have it witnessed by a person of standing and responsibility who had known her for some time. The only person she could think of was Mr Parsons, who owned the briquette factory where she was then working. Anyway he owed her a favour. He had once invited her into her office and before she could ask what he wanted had locked the door and unzipped his flies. 'If you can give it to the Yanks, Tessa, surely you can give it to me that's been so good to you, keeping you on in spite of reports about immorality?' Slavers were running down his double chins. She had been embarrassed because he had once told her he went to church every Sunday with his wife, but she had let him have his way, knowing that it would be over in half a minute.

She explained about the form and the photograph that had to be signed by him.

'I can't sign this,' he said, indignantly. 'It wouldn't be right.'

'What do you mean, Mr Parsons? It's legal.'

'This Yank you say wants to marry you, he must be off his head.'

'What right have you to say that, Mr Parsons?'

'Because you're nothing but a wee whure, Tessa Gilliespie, and only a man that's off his head would want to marry a whure.'

Still she was patient. 'That's nae business of yours, Mr Parsons.'

'If I sign this and help you to get to America then it is my business.'

She had had enough. 'Just sign the bluidy thing and shut your trap. Do you want me to turn up at the kirk door next Sunday and tell your wife you had me here in your office, against that wa'?'

The calendar that had been knocked off during that brief frantic affair had been replaced askew.

'You're a brazen wee bitch,' he muttered.

'If I have to be, Mr Parsons. Sign it, please.'

He signed it and then, not in the least surprising her for there was little about the sexual greed and cunning of men that she didn't know, he wanted her to let him do it again.

'You're forgetting I'm engaged, Mr Parsons.'

'You're also fired.'

She sent in the form, with the two photographs and the money. Back came a passport.

Next she had to get a visa. She decided it would be more prudent not to go in person to the American consulate in Edinburgh. The officials there, seeing and hearing her, might refuse to let her into America. So she wrote away for the necessary form, filled it in, and sent it back with her passport. She gave as her reason for wanting to go to America her intention to marry Harry. She enclosed his letter as proof.

The passport came back with the visa stamped on it.

3

Robert and Billy went with her in a taxi to St Enoch Square, where she would take the bus for Prestwick Airport. Her mother was still drunk after last night's farewell party.

If she had any regret at leaving it was because of Roberta. The girl was simple-minded, with a well-developed body. She had already been used by most of the boys in the street and not a few of the men. She would become a street-walker that did her business in closes and against lampposts. But even if I stayed, thought Tessa, I couldn't help her much. Whereas when I'm settled in America I can send for her.

She did not really believe that. Only somebody not right in the head like a saint would send for poor Roberta.

As for Billy, he had already been in the hands of the police for breaking and entering, and assault. She suspected that he took money from his pals for letting them have a shot at his sister, and she wouldn't have been surprised to learn that he took his turn. She was afraid of him, to tell the truth. 'Leave the boy alone,' her mother had told her. 'He means nae herm.' No harm, only incest, pimping, theft, and maybe murder one day.

She gave them a pound each. 'Don't you take your sister's, you fly wee bugger,' she said.

He winked evilly.

She waved to them from the bus. She had tears in her eyes. Roberta was weeping. Billy put his fingers to his nose.

It was up to her, she thought vaguely, to raise the standards of her family. She did not so much mind their not being respectable, but she wished that they could be more affectionate.

She admitted that she herself might be partly to blame. Her own childhood had been grim. At the age of ten she had been raped by one of her mother's fancy men. At school most of her teachers had treated her with contempt because she came from one of the most notorious families in the district and proved it every day by being pert and defiant. Her pertness and defiance had been necessary defences.

Without feeling in the least sorry for herself she knew that she had not been given a fair chance when a child. No one had ever shown her kindness. Her mother's female cronies had bought her sweets and given her cuddles, but only when they were drunk. Sober, they'd hardly looked at her because, she realised as she got older, they were ashamed. The shame people felt fascinated her. From an early age she had vowed never to feel any herself, and she never had.

In America she would start again. She would be Mrs Harry Folger, not Tessa Gilliepsie. If she had to use less make-up and wear not so bright clothes and cut her nails and watch her language and to go to bed with no man but her husband, well then she would. She might sometimes regret having to give up her talent for making men happy, but as a compensation she could have children and show them love.

4

It was the first time she had ever flown and the first time she had travelled to a foreign country. Both experiences she accepted calmly and with enjoyment.

On the plane she was a model passenger, keeping her seat-belt fastened, sleeping a good part of the way, going to the toilet only when it became necessary, hiding whatever nervousness she felt, eating all the food that was offered her, making no demands of the stewardesses, and remaining in her seat as requested at Los Angeles airport though many other passengers were standing up.

In the airport she went out with her suitcase to where people were gathered to meet friends and relatives.

There was no sign of Harry.

'Can you trust him, Tessa?' Cissie had asked. 'I don't mean he'll let you doon, though he might. I meant he might forget to turn up or mistake the date. Whit I'm really saying, Tessa, withoot offence, he cannae be very bright, can he?'

'Bright enough for me, Cissie,' she had replied.

As she stood there waiting, with her suitcase at her feet, she did not feel scared. She was sure he would come. She had expected him to be late. He was one of life's latecomers, unlike her who was always early. But even if he didn't come she knew where he lived and could find her way there. If he had gone back on his word and now didn't want to marry her and she was alone therefore in this country where she knew nobody she would still not be scared. She hadn't enough money for her return fare but if necessary she could earn it. Already she had been given the glad eye by three men, one of them black.

He was two and a half hours late. Never very wise-like at the best of times he looked particularly gawky as he tried to explain and apologise. He had quite a way to come and his car had broken down.

'Don't worry about it,' she said. 'You're here now.'

'You're looking great, Tessa,' he said.

He gazed at her fondly. With his small close eyes and his mouth that had a habit of suddenly falling open a lover's gaze did not suit him, but probably it didn't suit her either with her mouth that was too firm and her eyes that were too bright. Not that she was gazing at him all that fondly. It wasn't that she was angry with him for being late. She had already forgiven him for that. It was just that there in the airport with many strangers watching wasn't the place for intimate looks. Besides, there were things to be done and she was tired.

'Is it all right now?' she asked, meaning his car.

'Sure.'

'Where is it?'

'Parked just outside.'

'Let's go then.'

'Wouldn't you like a cup of coffee first?'

'No, thank you. I would like us to get on our way.'

She had expected an old banger but no, his car was fairly new though very dusty. It was big and swanky. She would have to learn to drive.

'Well, when do we get married?' she asked, as soon as they were in the car. She had decided to speak proper all the time.

'It'll take a day or two, Tessa.'

'Why?'

'We've got to get blood tests first.'

'What for?'

'To make sure we're healthy, I guess.'

'You mean, that we haven't got VD?'

'I guess so.'

'Well, I haven't.' Sadie had once caught a dose. It was Tessa who had made her go to a clinic. 'Have you?'

'No, no.'

'How far are we from Las Vegas?'

'Vegas? About six hours' drive, I guess.'

'Could we get married there without fuss?'

'I guess so, but it'd be after midnight before we got there.'

'Isn't Las Vegas open for business twenty-four hours of the day?'

'The casinos are. I don't know about the churches.'

'They're not really churches, they're just places where people can get married in a hurry. They'll be open. Right, Harry, head for Vegas.'

'But you must be tired, Tessa. Wouldn't tomorrow do?'

'No, it would not. I can get some sleep on the way.'

'If that's what you want, Tessa.'

'That's what I want, Harry.'

202

She could not have said why it was so important to her
to get married at once. She did not distrust him. She was
not usually impatient, and she was in no position to object
to pre-marital sex.

'You're the boss, Tessa. We can stop somewhere for a bite
to eat.'

He looked less gawky already.

She did not feel conceited about the good effect she was
having on him. He was having just as good an effect on her.
She felt more relaxed.

5

The big car was so comfortable, Harry drove so considerately,
and she was so tired, that though she wanted to stay awake
and keep him company she soon fell sound asleep.

She was awakened by his hand stroking her cheek.

'Whit is it?' she said, thinking for a moment she was
back in the briquette factory, in the corner where she had
used to snatch some sleep on a mattress of dirty sacks,
among mice.

'That's Vegas ahead, Tessa. I thought you'd like to see it
all lit up.'

'Thanks, Harry.' Yawning, she looked down on a sight she
had often seen in films but never had hoped to see in reality.
She felt she was dreaming. She wished Cissie and Sadie were
there to share her rapture.

They drove slowly along the famous Strip. It was like
fairyland, she thought, with all those millions of coloured
lights changing patterns all the time. If she had had plenty
of money she would have lived there all her life. What a
difference from Vorlich Street?

Whatever happened from now on she would never be

the same Tessa Gilliespie. She had come too far and seen wonders.

'You must be hungry,' said Harry. 'Would you like to eat first?'

'We'll celebrate afterwards. But I'd like to go to the lavatory. I expect there'll be a ladies' in the church.'

There was, and counting the ten minutes she spent in it the whole thing took less than half an hour. The ceremony would have disappointed Cissie who dreamt of a long white dress, armfuls of lilies, and a church as big as Glasgow Cathedral. But it suited Tessa. Like herself the two paid witnesses were yawning, the Justice of the Peace smelled of whisky and had a withered flower in his buttonhole, and the ring was exorbitantly dear, but it was all legal and binding.

Afterwards they drove to the Stardust Hotel where after booking a room they had dinner in the dimly lit restaurant. It was Tessa who ordered a bottle of wine and proposed a toast to Mr and Mrs Harry Folger.

On their way to their room they passed through the vast casino, Tessa was too thrifty to be much of a gambler but she tried a few machines. She lost all her nickels.

It didn't matter. She was going to be lucky in more important things.

About one o'clock, hand-in-hand, a honeymoon couple, they reached their room. It was by far the loveliest room Tessa had ever slept in. It had a large double bed. She had asked for this. She was aware of her obligations.

She had made love as a whore a good many times but never once as a wife. She knew there ought to be a difference. As a whore she had done her best and been paid in drinks and money, as a wife she would have to do her best too, for she would expect to be paid not only in money and property, half of all that Harry owned, but also in a lifetime of devotion and loyalty. She had never, like Sadie and Cissie sometimes, taken a scunner at the strange face pressing down on her, but at the same time she had never felt obliged to feel that every inch of the man on top of her or under her, even the pimples on his chin and the scars of old boils on his behind, were precious to her. She must feel that about her husband.

After it was over, with Harry snoring happily, well pleased with his bargain, she lay beside him aching in body and mind with the supreme effort she had exerted on his behalf. She hoped the silly soul wouldn't expect the same every night.

She thought about him. He was a stranger really. She had never met his father and mother and never would for they were both dead. He, thank goodness, wasn't likely to meet hers. She knew nothing about his childhood and he, again thank goodness, knew nothing about hers. She didn't know what size of shirt he took or what foods he especially liked. There were dozens of things they didn't know about each other, and if she could help it he'd remain ignorant till the day he died about many of those concerning her. Even if under her direction he became a loving husband he still wouldn't want to know that she had been raped when a child of ten, or that she had been enjoyed by at least sixteen sailors, though this surely he must suspect. It was an unspoken agreement between them never to mention it.

One thing he'd soon learn about her was that she didn't like sleeping naked. She didn't mind making love naked but she liked to sleep in a clean nightgown. She was naked now, like Harry, and felt uncomfortable; indeed, she couldn't get to sleep because of it. Tenderly disentangling her head from his arm she slipped out of bed and put on the new nightgown she had laid in readiness over a chair. It wasn't see-through. It was soft and white, embroidered with little coloured flowers. She felt virtuous in it. Putting it on was like regaining chastity. If Harry awoke and wanted more love-making she would put him off, as delicately as she could.

6

She would have been delighted to stay in Las Vegas for a day or two seeing all the sights, but Harry had promised the man looking after the gas station and store that he would be back that day before one o'clock. She believed promises should be kept. So after a little early morning love-making they got up, checked out, and drove to Denny's for breakfast.

It was a beautiful sunny morning. The stony hills in the distance were a mixture of colours, pink, purple, blue and violet.

She was wearing what she considered sensible clothes for a long car journey, red pants with a white top, green cardigan and boots with heels of medium height. She had on her bra with the most padding. It was hardly to deceive Harry, but she didn't want other men to be sorry for him with a wife whose breasts were so small. It had always seemed to her childish the way American men slobbered over big breasts. Look at Cissie McDade. She had whoppers. Yet in bed she must have been about as exciting as a bag of feathers. More than one sailor had been cured of this fetish after sampling first big-bosomed Cissie and then flat-chested Tessa.

She warned herself that she must dismiss these memories of herself and the sailors. She was not ashamed of them. She had consoled many a homesick man, cheered up gloomy ones, and given confidence to self-doubters. But she had now begun a new life. In Harry's home town there might be times, in the first year or two anyway, when she would feel bad about having to let her gift go to waste, but it would have to be done. There would be other things to take up her attention, children for instance. She wouldn't be surprised if she turned out to be just as good at bringing up children.

Harry seemed a little ill-at-ease that morning, especially whenever she asked him about Anglia. If she hadn't been feeling indulgent towards him she wouldn't have let him away with those mumbled evasions. They were caused after all by the slowness and, to be truthful, the dimness of his mind. As she had admitted to Cissie and Sadie he would never have wanted to marry her if he had had any brains. It didn't matter. She had enough brains for them both, in spite of what her teachers used to tell her. Their children needn't be brainless. Therefore, during breakfast and later in the car, when he nodded or shook his head like a dummy she curbed her impatience, patted his hand, and gave up her questioning about Anglia. After all in about four hours she would see it for herself.

It was marvellous driving out of Las Vegas along the wide sunny road, seated beside her husband in their own car, but it was not amazing. She had always thought of herself as someone special to whom one day this kind of adventure would happen. Every time she had watched a romantic film or read a romantic story it had been easy for her to imagine herself in the heroine's place. True, she was never as beautiful but she always had ten times more gumption and enterprise. Often the heroine could have saved herself a lot of trouble if she had simply let the villain rape her. If the hero had objected she would have been entitled to tell him to go and raffle himself, since he hadn't been there when needed. In any case the villain was usually more interesting than the hero.

That morning *she* was the heroine. As the hero, Harry was not as handsome as he might have been but his being so big-eared and slow-witted had the advantage that he was modest and left all the decisions to her.

She pretended that there was a loaded revolver in the glove compartment. Somewhere ahead, waiting to kidnap her, was

the big, brawny, black-moustached, well-hung villain. She
would shoot herself rather than let him rape her.

Like hell she would!

No woman in the whole of America knew better than
Tessa Gilliespie, now Mrs Folger, how silly all this was but
that didn't stop her from enjoying it.

They drove through the industrial town of Henderson.
Tall chimneys smoked.

'I hope Anglia isn't like this,' she said.

Harry shook his head.

It was certainly the right country for mystery and adventure,
all shimmering desert and faraway hazy mountains. Once she
thought she saw in the distance a large lake. It was a salt flat,
Harry said.

At last the desert began to worry her. There was too much
of it. There was nothing else but it.

She said so.

'There's a lot to be seen in the desert, Tessa.'

'A lot of dirt and stones.'

'What about those Joshua trees?'

'Those prickly ones like arms pointing?'

He smiled. 'The Mormons thought they were pointing
the way to the promised land, like Joshua in the Bible.'

'That's silly. They're all pointing in different directions.
You're not a Mormon yourself, by any chance?'

'No. They're really a kind of lily. Would you believe that,
Tessa? In the spring when their white flowers are out they're
beautiful.'

'Who are you kidding?'

'It's true, Tessa. You'll see.'

'I can't wait. What else besides Joshua trees?'

'Creosote bushes. Paper-bag bushes. Cigarette plants. Brittle-
brush. And lots of small flowers. In the spring when they're
all in bloom the desert's really something.'

She sneered, sceptically. Yet she was surprised and moved by his enthusiasm. He really seemed to like the desert. Odd, considering that he had been a sailor.

'What about animals?' she asked. 'Nothing but snakes, I should think.'

'Not so many snakes. Kit foxes. Kangaroo rats. Coyotes. Lizards. Chuckwallahs.'

'What are chuckwallahs?'

'Lizards that blow themselves up so you can't poke them out of holes. They eat plants. Other lizards eat insects. In the mountains yonder you'll find flocks of big-horned sheep.'

'You seem to know a lot about the desert.'

'So I should, Tessa. I've been about it most of my life. I used to go hunting when I was a kid. By myself mostly. I stayed out for days.'

Again she was moved. He seemed to have been lonely as a child. 'At night too?'

'It's best at night.'

'How can it be best if you can't see it?'

'You can see it. By the light of the stars. Wait till you see how bright the stars are, Tessa.'

'It's street lamps I like to see bright, thank you very much.'

They stopped for gas at a place she wouldn't even have called a village, it was so small. On the bleak hills round about were abandoned gold mines.

'What's this place called?' she asked.

'Searchlight.'

She had to laugh. 'Why is it called that?'

'I don't know. Would you like something to eat or drink?'

'No, but I'd like to stretch my legs.'

'Put on your coat. We're high up here.'

He was right. The air was cold after the warmth of the

car. As she walked about she saw a battered pick-up truck pull up outside a cafe. Out of it stepped stiffly a little old man at whom she gazed in wonder. In her day she had seen dozens of Wild West films. Here they were all embodied in this old man with the long beard, cowboy hat, and calf-length high-heeled boots. On the side of the truck was painted his name: Cactus Jack. He would live alone in some shack in the midst of the wilderness, looking for gold.

She would have hated such a life herself but she was grateful to him for doing it. Though she had little experience of the world she liked to think of it as having great variety.

They drove on.

'Have you got a map?' she asked.

'I'm sorry, Tessa. I forgot to bring one.'

'It doesn't matter. I'll look out for sign-posts.'

Not long after leaving Searchlight they crossed the state border into California. Tessa felt pleased. Already she thought of California as her home state.

At last came the sign-post she was waiting for. It indicated a side road that led to a place called Amboy and then to Anglia. Anglia was still 75 miles away. They should be there in about two hours.

She began to feel excited.

7

After leaving Amboy (which was smaller even than Searchlight) the road, straight as an arrow, out through desert so sandy that the road in places was covered. Far ahead was a gap in the mountains. Beyond it lay Anglia and surely the last of the desert.

The road was empty. No cars overtook them. None were behind them. Only one passed coming the other way.

She noticed Harry was driving more slowly. Knowing nothing about cars, she wondered at first if he was afraid his tyres would burst. Then she realised it must be because he was now close to home.

They were now through the gap and yet it was still all desert. She could see no sign anywhere of town or village. The desert was flat and stretched as far as she could see in every direction, to hills on the horizon. The only road was the one they were travelling on. Anyone wanting to reach those hills, if anyone was crazy enough, would have to walk or drive over the desert. She had a picture in her mind of old Cactus Jack making for the hills.

Then she saw, in the distance, a freight train, very very long, pulled by three engines. It did not alleviate the loneliness, it made it worse.

By the side of the road appeared a wooden shack, painted green. At first she thought it was abandoned. The notice COLD BEER could be long out of date. But there was a signpost which said: East Anglia. Pop. 10. Elevation 1425.

Before she could give vent to her astonishment, disbelief, indignation, and alarm, they arrived at Anglia proper. Here the signpost said: Anglia. Pop. 25. Elevation 1426.

It must be wrong. Even twenty-five people would need at least four houses. She could see only one and it wasn't really a house at all, it was the ramshackle store behind the small gas station. There were also two sheds, one red and the other green, both in a state of ruin. About them were scattered the rusty carcasses of cars.

There was so much sky it frightened her.

They stopped outside the store. An old man with a face so brown she thought he must be a Red Indian came out to greet them.

She looked at Harry. He scratched his nose and stared at a fly on the windscreen.

'Is this it?' she asked.

He nodded.

She said no more but got out.

She was too numbed for anger. Ignoring the old man she walked to the back of the store where there was a door marked WOMEN. She went in, wiped the seat with a piece of toilet paper, lowered her pants, sat down, and thoughtfully emptied her bladder. Here was the worst crisis in her life. She didn't want to confront it with crossed legs. Anyway, she could think better in a lavatory, provided it wasn't too smelly, and to be fair this one wasn't.

Outside she heard Harry and the old man talking. She also heard the freight train rattle past. Evidently the line came quite close to the store. When she got bored she could always wave to the engine-driver.

She would sue Harry for false pretences. No, that was daft, she'd need a lawyer and money. Besides, Harry had never praised Anglia, it had been the desert he had praised. He had told her that Anglia didn't have many supermarkets, and it hadn't; that it didn't have as many swimming-pools as Palm Springs, and it didn't; and that it had no airport, which it certainly hadn't. There had been no false pretences on his part, only false hopes on hers.

She tried to see it from his point of view. He had married her knowing she was little better than a whore. He had given her respectability. That was worth more than a swimming-pool. Also in some ways Anglia was an improvement on Vorlich Street, it had more space, fresher air, and more sunshine; it was also much quieter.

The question she had to answer, and she was going to sit there smoking until she had answered it honestly, was would she have come all the way to America to marry him if she had known that Anglia was just a gas station in the middle of the desert, a Men's and a Women's (with room for one customer at a time), two broken-down sheds, a collection of wrecked cars, and an enormous sky?

She inspected her face in the cracked mirror. It needed some attention. With shaky hand she applied lipstick, powder, and scent. The scent had been a parting gift from Sadie and Cissie. Thinking of them she almost broke down and wept. She never felt sorry for herself but there were times when she wished somebody would feel sorry for her. Here there was only Harry and he would have a fucking cheek to be sorry for her.

She went out into the bright cool air. Harry and the old man were chatting beside a truck even more ancient than Cactus Jack's.

She approached them. Harry introduced the old man as Pete. It seemed to her that Pete's frank blue eyes appraised her as being too skinny and made-up for a place like Anglia.

She didn't say a word.

Soon Pete climbed into his truck and drove away, across the road and on to the desert on the other side, in clouds of dust. Probably his shack was miles away.

'So long, neighbour,' she murmured.

She and Harry were alone in Anglia. No cars passed on the road. Neither the shop nor the gas station could be said to be doing brisk business.

Harry asked if she would like to see the living quarters.

'In a minute,' she said.

She wanted to, well, she just didn't know what she wanted to do. To shut her eyes and scream? To claw up a handful of Harry's fucking desert and throw it in his face? To weep and beg him to give her the money to go back home? To laugh?

She went round to the back of the store, leaned against it, lit another cigarette, shivered a little, shaded her eyes against the brilliant sun, and laughed.